EVA

EVASION

Françoise Sagan

translated by Elfreda Powell

This edition published in Great Britain in 1994 by
Allison & Busby
an imprint of Wilson & Day Ltd
5 The Lodge
Richmond Way
London W12 8LW

First published in hardback by Severn House Publishers Ltd 1993

Translated from the original French
Les Faux-Fuyants
Published by Julliard, Paris, 1991

Copyright © by Francoise Sagan 1991
Translation copyright © 1993 by Elfreda Powell

The moral right of the author is asserted

A catalogue record for this book is available from the British Library

ISBN 0 74900 138 0

Printed and bound in Great Britian by
Cox & Wyman Ltd, Reading, Berkshire

"With hard work and perseverance, all difficulties can be overcome."

Virgil

"He who harvests in June reaps a storm."

old proverb from The Beauce region

Chapter 1

The limousine – a Chenard-Walcker – looked dazzling in the bright June sunshine of 1940, and the horde of dusty, noisy vehicles jammed in front and behind, and sometimes alongside in another queue, emphasized its splendour. The whole convoy was crawling along the Route Nationale, which had become too narrow to contain it, and was punctuated with scraggy, greyish trees; every so often the road was blasted by furious, frenzied gunfire from the Stukas, and constantly – and just as violently – by the summer sun.

"This must be the most clapped-out collection of cars on the French roads," Bruno Delors said. He was the youngest, but the greatest snob even so, of the four seated in the back of the limousine.

"Well, of course. Anyone who could left eight days ago." Diane Lessing was the oldest, richest and bossiest of the four.

Hanging around while France collapsed seemed to her as inexcusable as being late for the opening night at Bayreuth, as she made plain in her severe tone.

"Yes, a good week ago," Loïc said, backing her up. For thirty years Loïc Lhermitte had been an attaché at the Quai d'Orsay, and it was as such that he intervened.

1

He was offering only a tactical viewpoint of their flight from the capital: here, as in his other opinions, *any* criterion seemed preferable to a moralistic one.

"It's all my fault," the fourth passenger, Luce Ader, moaned. Aged twenty seven' Luce had a super-rich – and absent – husband, and hence Bruno Delors as her lover for the past two years.

She had just had an operation for appendicitis, which was incongruous enough at twenty-seven and even more so in June 1940. Her appendicitis had delayed her departure from Paris, as well as her friends' and her lover's.

Diane Lessing had been waiting for an old friend, an English peer, to collect her in his biplane which had never arrived; doubtless it had been mobilized *en route*. Likewise Loïc Lhermitte had been counting on leaving in a friend's car and at the very last moment had had to give up his seat to a nearer relative or someone more important. Both Loïc and Diane, who had been stranded in Paris with no trains, no cars, and no means of transport, had seen their fondness for Luce grow. They had hovered over her as she convalesced, and climbed aboard her superb Chenard-Walcker only at the last moment, along with her lover. And now, after all these hazards, they were heading for Lisbon where Luce's husband was waiting with a reward for their devotion: a bunk for each of them on board the ship he had chartered to New York.

"No darling, it's not your fault," Diane cried. "Don't be stupid, you mustn't torture yourself' Luce. There was nothing you could have done about it," she added with a small commendatory smile.

2

"In any case Luce, as I've already said, without you, I'd be on foot," Loïc added in an attempt to go one better.

Long ago he had recognized the importance of these shabby admissions, which he felt deserved instant praise for their self-mockery and wit, and might in the future earn praise for their honesty, should the need arise. His remark brought a nervous laugh from Diane and Bruno' who were inclined to forget that from time to time Loïc was treated by the society he frequented as totally insignificant, because he had no money.

For all that, Loïc really liked Luce Ader and would have done quite a lot for her, including staying in her comfortable apartment, watching the German troops file past, which in any other circumstance would have frightened him a great deal.

"Oh, come now, Luce," Bruno said. "That's simply not true. You know perfectly well it wasn't just for love of you Diane turned down Percy Dorset's plane. You know that. And I can understand her . . . Those small private planes are horribly dangerous I find."

Bruno Delors came from a good family which had recently fallen on hard times. He had been broken in and harnessed to all the conventions of snobbery and was completely bewitched by them, but, deprived of the material means of practising them, he had declared himself a gigolo with all the aggressive conviction of someone intent on revenge, and no one had dared tell him it was not a profession to be proud of. Which was why he treated the women who kept him, badly, as if by exploiting them – with a certain amount of success – he was merely reimbursing

3

himself for what society had stolen from his family.

In the two years he had lived with (and off) Luce Ader, he had lost some of his drive. Luce's innocence, her total ignorance about money and her lack of vanity inhibited him from being as brutal with her as he had liked to be with other women. Naturally he bore her a grudge, but how could he take it out on someone who did not know what she "possessed"? How could he steal from someone who gave everything away? And since he didn't hold the balance of power, he was currently either in a bad temper or plain disagreeable, which was astonishing for a boy like him, who until then had merely been a frivolous, spiteful go-getter.

And so it was that, imprudently, he let slip his insolent remarks to Diane, which Luce might have tolerated, but not the famous Madame Lessing.

"Are you saying I waited for Luce because I was afraid of aeroplanes? That would have been quite idiotic, with these Stukas machine-gunning from morning till night."

"I'm not claiming anything, my dear Diane," Bruno said raising his hands. "God spare me. I've never made any claims in regard to you." And he added: "To your regret I hope."

He winked at Luce. Poor sod, thought Loïc. Diane smiled forbearingly, her eyes remote.

"As far as that's concerned, my dear Bruno, it's not God who'll spare you, it's me. First of all I'm too old for that sort of . . . distraction . . . and more to the point I've always preferred slim men . . ."

She laughed. Bruno began to laugh with her.

4

"I must admit, Diane, I'd never hoped to seduce you, even if you were a consenting party."

"Ah well, there you're wrong. Think about it. In ten years' time, for example, I'll still be the same age . . . at worst in my seventies. But, as for you, you'll be forty. Am I right? And, dear Bruno, I can't really say if you'll be young enough for me at forty. At your time of life and in your position, one ages much more quickly than at mine. Believe me.

"It can be very tiring, you know, to have to go on pleasing for such a long time," she added sympathetically.

There was a silence. Bruno had turned red and Luce who had not understood – or who yet again was pretending not to, either out of cowardice or boredom (Loïc still could not work out which was the more likely) – began yelping like an agitated pup.

"What's going on between you two? I don't follow you. What's the matter. . . ?"

"Nothing's going on," Loïc said. "Now, if you'll excuse me, I'm going to stretch my legs, I need some exercise . . ."

He got out of the Chenard-Walcker and began walking along the verge.

All this small-minded sniping and aggressive prattle had to stop, he thought. Better to be gunned down than die genteelly. The whole of France was already falling apart, if the veneer cracked too, they were done for. Loïc experienced a sudden pride at his thought that the veneer, for all its superficiality and vanity, for all its frequent comparison with snobbery or hypocrisy, and the ridicule so often piled upon it, would enable him to

5

die with as much modesty and courage as the heroism other men of better quality died with in battle. Having said that, young Bruno had asked for it. Diane could easily turn savage in such a situation. Loïc smiled. He had to admit he would have done just the same.

After years of living in Paris, a witty remark had assumed supreme power, it had become an irresistible passport, which transgressed all laws, including those of kindness, and decency, and even personal ambition. Loïc was among those who were prepared to ruin their career for the sake of a witty remark. But they were fast becoming a rare breed, since most men had now turned their "business affairs" into the only kind of "affair" that mattered. It was happening in Europe now just as much as in America.

A child stepped on his toes, stumbled against him, then fell over in the grass and began to wail. From the car where she sat sweating in the sun, the child's mother cast him a look of hatred, and Loïc turned back. It was decidedly better to take refuge in that small wickedly luxurious cocoon, than slog it out on this bourgeois moralistic road.

Ever since they'd left Paris and for many, many kilometres, their sumptuous limousine had provoked rude remarks from other fugitives whom they slowly overtook and who then overtook them, as one or other lane of traffic moved. Gradually the heat, the Stukas, the bottlenecks, the disorganization and the terror obscured the pervading irony, particularly when the slowness of the convoy, the progressively growing queue of vehicles, then the obligatory halts, had ended up inflicting the same neighbours on everyone in front and behind. In the Chenard-Walcker's case, they had a car in front jam-packed with a huge, screaming family and, behind, a tiny vehicle belonging to a very elderly, loathsome couple who never exchanged a word. He opened the door. Bruno was still in his corner having the sulks; Luce and Diane were wittering away.

"Don't you think the countryside is wonderful in spite of everything, Luce?" Diane was saying. "What a view. You never see that in Paris . . . And for good reason I'm sure you'll say. But it's true, isn't it, that in Paris one never has time to look out of the window? It's a different world, don't you think? Look out there, all that silence, that space, that – "

"Don't you dare say 'peace', Diane," Loïc said.

She began to laugh because in fact that was what she was just on the point of saying.

"Is there anything left to drink?" she asked.

Loïc turned towards the motionless chauffeur behind the glass partition and tapped on it, before abruptly turning to Bruno, who was still in a surly mood.

"Listen, old chap. Would you mind seeing to this? Is that all right?"

Then he turned to the women who were watching him curiously. Oh well, yes, it probably did seem odd that he, the so courteous, attentive, obliging Loïc, a man in his fifties, had no qualms about delegating his domestic chores to a gigolo of thirty. But it wasn't so outrageous as all that. In the meantime the chauffeur had lowered the glass panel. Bruno spluttered.

"André . . . Jean . . . We're hungry. Have you got the hamper with you?"

7

"Yes, of course, Monsieur. Would Monsieur like me to bring it round to the back?"

"Yes, do that, would you? Yes, perfect. That would be perfect," Diane yapped. "And will you have something Jean? Then you won't be disrupted while you're driving. It's curious how travelling makes one hungry, isn't it?" she added as she slid her bloodred varnished nails between two buttons on her blouse.

The chauffeur had opened the rear door, and placed the hamper on the carpet between Loïc and Diane's feet, and was now trying to push it a little further in among the passengers; but Diane had suddenly drawn her knees together and wedged the basket between her calves, gripping it like a football.

"Leave it there," she said. "It isn't bothering me, I assure you; my legs aren't so long as Luce's as you know. I know I'm extremely slim and the fashion nowadays is for American-style carthorses, but it wasn't always so; there was a time when *petite* models were highly successful. Believe me," she said as she now addressed a strange, invisible, fascinated interviewer whom she sometimes invented when her audience showed too little interest in her conversation.

All this time she was fumbling with her beringed hand inside the hamper, and at the end of her speech she triumphantly withdrew a bottle of white wine along with a corkscrew.

"Luce," she said, brandishing the bottle. "Have a drop of um . . . (she looked at the label) a drop of Ladoucette."

"No, no thanks."

Three hours and fifty kilometres earlier they had

stopped at one of those medieval-style inns that can be found near the Route Nationale, whose proprietor, apparently resisting current events, had insisted on making them try his *foie gras*. And so they had only left the table two hours ago, and since then, Diane had already eaten two hard-boiled eggs, but was still hungry.

"Honestly, I do wonder where you can put all that food." Bruno whistled between his white teeth and ran his gaze down Diane's bony body. "I don't know where you've tucked all that away, but all the same, well done."

"I've always been a woman who burns up her calories as she goes along," said Diane with an experienced air, apparently quite happy with her meagre figure. "I hope you can do the same."

Their car took off again suddenly and Diane who had been sitting on the edge of the seat, made a grab for the velvet handle beside her, missed and was thrown backwards; right to the back of her seat, arms and legs waving in an attempt to find her balance, and with such gracelessness that both men inwardly laughed.

It was then that they heard a woman's piercing scream: "They're coming, they're coming." And the screams mounted.

"So you find cars safer, do you, Bruno?" Diane had time to remark as she instinctively ducked her head . . .

For "they", as they now knew, were German Stukas and their machine-guns.

"Stop, Jean! stop!"

Bruno tapped a little too hard on the glass partition

9

separating them to ask the chauffeur to park on the verge, but he hadn't heard.

"I don't want to die with these people," Loïc thought. "I haven't lived till fifty and more to die with cartoon characters like these," he told himself once again, for they had already been fired on twice since they left Paris.

While Luce and Diane lay on the floor of the car, he and Bruno gallantly lay on top of them as protection.

Unfortunately for Loïc, he was lying hard up against Diane's heap of aristocratic bones and he groaned, and continued to grumble to himself. This is what thirty years of obeying the dictates of Society has reduced me to, thirty years of docile, even-tempered behaviour and enforced celibacy. For Loïc's salary from the Quai d'Orsay gave him enough to live on, but not in the world he loved, which was as necessary to him as oxygen. As a consequence, for thirty years he'd been included in Society on the grounds of his personal qualities, and also because he could be fourteenth at table, make up a foursome at bridge, be an instant escort for whatever widow, divorcee or spinster happened to need one. And it was almost out of human respect that gradually Society had come to think of him as Loïc Lhermitte, the charming homosexual. How else to explain his bachelorhood? When he met a woman he liked and who liked him – a not uncommon experience – he had to invent something to prevent him from having the normal fate of a normal man, a fate which would have cost him his invitations to Society parties . . . In fact he had abandoned his prejudices too late, refused for too long to live at the expense of a woman he might

10

have loved, perhaps because he lacked simplicity, but mostly through fear that such a woman might herself lack simplicity; just as he had refused to live in the clutches of a woman he might not have loved. And here the real reason was lack of energy when faced with the long unremitting obligation that his existence would have become.

"My God!" another voice called from outside. A voice in the process of breaking – or had it changed pitch through fear . . .? But a voice, in any case, that fear had rendered asexual. "My God! They're coming back. There're masses of them," it cried, then it stopped.

And quite suddenly the road became totally silent. Theatrically silent. Naturally it was Diane who broke the spell.

"It's so hot," she murmured into the floor covering. "Are you sure th . . ."

"Shush!" Loïc whispered stupidly. As if a pilot could have heard them and targeted them. But, above, he could just hear that repellent beelike drone which they had already heard twice, three times, that day, so faint to start with, but persisting for three or four seconds without growing any louder. Just as if it were done so that people would get used to the droning and drop their guard . . . Then all at once the buzzing grew stronger and more ferocious and burst into the air, as if the plane had broken its moorings and suddenly dropped from the sky. The noise swelled gigantically, obscenely, filling the countryside all around them: all that emptiness, that silence . . . He saw the buzzing growing in his neighbour's eyes, withering, tearing the

11

green grass near his face; it became a savage outrageous apocalyptic clamour, clinging to the ground, burying in it miserable hunched-up human bodies: packets of skin filled with flesh, blood and nerves, drowning in water, packets that were supposed to think and feel and which now thought nothing and felt nothing and were nothing but a horrified vacuum, as centuries before, their ancestors had been under this same sun, a sun which must have laughed at the pretensions of these people in times of peace, at the sickness they felt when confronted by their fear of dying.

Something hit the side of the car, shook it, and overturned it, so that it now lay on its side, taking with it its obsequious and docile passengers, who cavorted through the air, inflicting blows on one another as they passed, but soundlessly. For the only word which came into their heads was a silently screamed "No!" An imprecise "No" addressed to no one in particular, with no reproach, almost no surprise and no bitterness, a "No" which was the sole product of millions of brain cells in their millions of circumvolutions.

Just as pain generally does, the noise died quickly, more quickly than it had come. The Stukas flying six at a time had never flown so low or been so ferocious. Machine-gunning unarmed civilians all along the roads had certainly been promised by the Nazis, and was something the Quai d'Orsay had dreaded for many long, secretive years. Loïc hated this war which had happened so quickly and was progressing so badly. He could perhaps have stayed on in Paris . . . tried to resist . . . what? . . . how? At his age? The receptions, the parties would still be there of course. But he was not sure he would have enjoyed them.

In Paris it was not a question of resistance but survival. Just as he was kicking Luce involuntarily in the stomach, as she was suddenly thrown towards him, and as he was tearing his head away from Diane's hands which were clinging to his hair for the second time, and while grasping the back of the seat with both hands to hold himself upright before the next disaster, Loïc suddenly recognized the clatter of a typewriter which had been pounding space and time while he was whirling around, and he shouted hoarsely to Diane and Luce. For the clatter belonged to a machine-gun. He should have been alarmed about it sooner (the machine-gun was wasting no time.)

Then somewhere a child began to cry and silence returned, a tense, vibrant silence . . . Loïc's first reflex was to get out of that accursed box, that metal and leather cage in which he had almost died. He fumbled around and found something which resembled a handle, shook it and felt the door on his side opening. He was about to slide out when a Christian reflex made him turn to Luce, who was undoubtledly still alive, since she was following him, and in decisive fashion for once.

The car was lying with one side tilted in the air, and he allowed himself to fall out on to the tarmac, where he came to rest against a helpful cushion. Luce, who had managed to stand up, caught sight of what had taken place behind Loïc, immediately turned away and gagged. Loïc skewed round, following her gaze, and discovered that his wonderful cushion was the chauffeur's body: poor Jean, who ten minutes earlier

13

had been passing them the hamper. He jolted upright, flinching away from his grim support, while, borne by its weight, the corpse slowly keeled over and toppled to the ground, face down. Loïc was now standing, livid with disgust, making helpless little gestures. It's horrible, he said to himself at last. I've *lived* through a moment of horror, true horror I've never experienced before. And if in the future anyone should mention the feeling of horror, it will be *this* moment I remember. But he did not react in the way he thought he should, and felt less horrified than hurt, stupid and confused at having withdrawn his shoulder from that pathetic corpse and let it fall lugubriously, pitifully, obscenely. All the while, his eyes were coldly surveying the scene (and he reproached himself for this, too), picking out the close, parallel, vaulting lines of machine-gun fire from the plane, which had scored and churned the edge of the ditch and the road in a meticulous geometric pattern, avoiding the old people's vehicle but drilling into the right wing, the hood and rear left of the limousine and finally crossing the road to an unknown destination, whipping up the tarmac, and killing Jean as it passed, who just chanced to be in its path. (A chance no more idiotic than all those fateful coincidences, but add to it the cruelty of war and the idea that "this" had been done on purpose, by some anonymous sadist in Munich or somewhere, and it became even more outrageously stupid and indecent.)

"Poor Jean," Luce said, and knelt beside the corpse with that ease women have with the wounded and the dead, in contrast to men who – like Loïc – instinctively moved away.

"Whatever's happened?" Diana called out as she appeared in front of the car like a second threatening attack, and, even though she could see Luce leaning over Jean's corpse, continued in her irritated voice:

"Will someone tell me what's happened?" she said, as though the facts, the blinding evidence before her very eyes were not enough, and she needed a few social niceties or comments, rather than reality, to bring home the message, and (as Loïc understood only too well) reassure her.

"God! What a load of filth those Stukas are," said Bruno who had come round from the other side and was looking at Luce kneeling, without daring to come closer. No doubt, like Loïc, he was offended by the act of death. And for a moment Loïc was overwhelmed at the idea of possibly having a reflex in common with a creature like him.

"Luce. Look. Do stand up. Can't you see there's nothing more we can do . . . What're we to do with him now?"

"He can't be left here, particularly with all these ants," Luce groaned.

Diane stared up at the sky for an answer, as though begging the heavens to bear witness to the unforeseen nuisance inflicted on them by having a chauffeur stuck somewhere other than in his seat behind the steering wheel.

"What're we to do with ourselves?" she sighed after a suitable pause.

"Do with ourselves?" Bruno said. "Well, I can drive."

And as if to prove it he kicked the nearside tyre, like a pro. But scarcely was he at the steering wheel than the Chenard-Walcker let off some loud bangs, and a thick smoke began pouring out.

Loïc was leaning towards the car when a calm drawling voice spoke from overhead, arousing every-one.

"You won't get far in that."

The voice came from the owner of a cart, drawn by two carthorses, which was attempting to cross the road at right angles between the old people's car and a heap of metal, which in its time had been a Chenard-Walcker (a Chenard-Walcker which, the summer before, had even represented its make in the 1939 Grand Prix for Sporting Elegance at Deauville. The Grand Prix trophy had been carried off in triumph by Madame André Ader, known as Luce to her friends, as reported at the time in the local *Gazette* and *Le Figaro*.)

"Monsieur, as you can see, we're in fact in something of a tight spot," Diane said in a friendly, somewhat benevolent manner, for some films on the Chouans – the royalist peasantry – had won her over to peas-ants. She also had a strong liking for tramps: she confessed to a lively compassion for their picturesque-ness, a curiosity as to how they could have reached the plight they were in, and an immense respect for their detachment from worldly possessions. She also professed the highest regard for working men, arti-sans, the liberal professions, shopkeepers, farmers, clerks, captains of industry and their assistants, the military and the NCOs, porters etc. And finally she had nothing against *concierges* – she found them quite affable. On the other hand she had only contempt and revulsion for the average Frenchman, particularly

16

when they formed groups among themselves, which when sufficiently large became a "crowd". A crowd so different from the people Diane venerated in her vague sort of way like certain crude, rustic implements of the Middle Ages: people who sat before their hearth in the evening, while the crowd, in a state of perpetual excitement, streamed along the boulevards.

The young peasant's expression changed from one of stupor to repugnance, then serenity tempered with a certain disdain for the disorder he saw. An expression which remained unaltered until he noticed the corpse lying by the roadside, and then which indicated a sort of confidence rather than horror, a sort of reassurance, as if he had at last found a point in common with this gaggle of strangers.

Chapter 2

The yokel was of medium build, his hair and eyes chestnut brown; he had a narrow, typically French face, with a prominent, fleshy nose above a shapely, impish mouth. His body, made lean and muscular through farm work, revealed a sturdy torso above narrow hips, and, as though stencilled on this tanned torso, was a spotlessly white vest.

Loïc, who valued virility in men above all else, could see at first glance that this young man was dangerous, particularly for a certain type of woman whose sensuality had been roused, or at least primed – and which definitely did not include Luce.

The three years it had taken her as a lonely, pretty and much courted woman to choose a lover – and then it had to be that cheesecake, that brutish mediocrity Bruno – left little room for hope in this area. Which was all for the best. It was no time to be playing Lady Chatterley, especially with Lord Chatterley-Ader waiting impatiently for them in Lisbon since the day before, to leave for America.

Diane's make-up was beginning to run in the sun, as she stared in a black rage at all the multi-coloured smoke pouring from the Chenard-Walcker, without seeing them. The farmer, who had finally managed to pass between the car with the huge family – whose begetter had reversed for him – and the remains of the limousine, was now very close.

"Ah! That be some smoke and no mistake," he said from the heights of his ramshackle cart, and took a cigarette from his pocket. "Whatever happened to it?"

Diane, always responsive to a new face, attempted a reply. "It was fired on from a plane . . . literally peppered with bullets . . . One of them must have hit a sensitive spot – a vital part of the engine I should think. In addition the water has evaporated. And in addition to that, it was a prototype, one of the first numbers in the series, and only poor Jean here could have repaired it."

As she spoke she pointed to the corpse of the aforesaid Jean, and the farmer shook his head sympathetically, which was nice of him. Here at least was someone practical as opposed to that buffoon Bruno. What was he up to now, bent over the steering wheel, jiggling the levers in all directions? A fine time to be jiggling levers. Really! You couldn't rely on Bruno' and still less on Loïc, who, she noted, was looking dead-eyed at this farmer. That was all one needed. The final straw.

In reality, Loïc was searching his memory for what play it was that their different attitudes reminded him of. He remembered: Racine's *Phaedra*, and Theramenes reciting "He was riding in his chariot . . ." Theramenes must be me, he thought. Luce is the beautiful Phaedra, Diane the wicked Œnone, while Theseus sternly awaits us in Lisbon. But what part

20

would the pathetic Bruno have? Aesthetically he should be Hippolytus, but, in the circumstances, and given his chariot was trying to avoid the Stukas, Hippolytus could only be this young farmer, attempting to escape the unleashed waves of Fate.

"What're you thinking about, Loïc?"

Œnone-Diane's voice seemed angry and impatient.

"This is no time for dreaming, my dear. What *are* we going to do with poor Jean here, who can't . . ." She stopped just before saying "who can't drive us any more" or "who's holding us up" or "who's no longer any use to anyone": all of which sprang naturally to mind, and decided on "who can't be left all alone by the roadside . . . Now, come on."

She was irritated.

"We've got to do something. And as for that other idiot down there, I don't know what on earth he's doing fiddling round with the car. Surely he doesn't think he can repair it now it's ablaze?"

"What d'you mean by 'that other idiot'? Are you implying I'm an idiot too?" Loïc asked.

"Oh, this is no time to take offence," she went on, without retracting her remark. "What about you, Luce, have you any ideas on how we can get out of this mess?"

She took a couple of steps and turned brusquely on poor dumbfounded Luce.

"After all, it's your car that got us into it," she reproached her.

"I'm sorry, but it was working really well before, you know," Luce said, stepping back.

"It was her car, but it wasn't her plane," Loïc, in

fairness, corrected Diane. "So let's forget this heap of scrap iron, shall we? Monsieur, please," he said firmly to the farmer, who was almost totally lost in thought, "Monsieur, would you be able to take our friend's body somewhere in your cart . . .?"

But he was cut short by Luce, now overflowing with fervour. She seemed on the point of clasping her hands in prayer and falling to her knees. What a wonderful Pietà she'd make, Diane thought in exasperation.

"Oh yes, Monsieur . . . Is there no church near by, or hospital . . .? Couldn't one find an ambulance to take poor Jean there?"

"And how d'you think this ambulance would get here?" Diane was fuming. "By flying the high wire? Or crossing the sea? And what could your hospital do? Can't you see it's too late for a hospital? And as for a church? Is it really important to be singing hymns in the present circumstances? No, you can't be serious, Luce. No way."

Literally stamping her foot, she turned to the farmer as the only person worth talking to.

"And what about the car? Is there really nothing more one can do about it?" Luce asked, innocent as ever.

"The car? Oh, that won't be no use to you no more," the farmer said.

And, as if to lend weight to his words, he shot a long stream of brownish saliva from the other side of his chariot. The two women shuddered and lowered their gaze, just as if, without warning, he had become completely naked before their very eyes. Loïc had felt the same, but was thinking: It's funny, but in spite of his mannerisms, there's nothing really shocking about this boy. I must talk to him man to man, a formula he rarely used. I must get my women away from here." He turned to his two travelling companions and saw they were exhausted, their clothes crumpled, make-up all awry, the one prattling, the other silent, but both wrecks. And a quite new feeling of compassion and protectiveness entered his mind. It's just as well that I'm here, he thought, with me as a Tarzan figure they're in safe hands.

"Now listen, Mesdames," he said in his old facetious tone, a relic of happier times when they went from party to party, drinking cocktails and joking about people who weren't there – "Go and see that hunk of a man in the car and tell him to unload the luggage: that would be most helpful. I meanwhile must talk to our new friend here. Go. Go."

There must have been authority in his voice for they obeyed. Meanwhile he sat coolly waiting on the step of the cart, astonished with how well his legs were carrying him.

"Tell me, old chap, you're not going to abandon me with these two poor women and the boy with the sulks are you? No, it's no joke . . . there are moments too hard to bear in a man's life."

The other man looked at him with his brownish, yellowish, greyish eyes – a weird colour in any case – and gave a quick smile. He had big, very white teeth, hardly stained by tobacco.

"No, I isn't going to leave you in this fix," he said. "Especially with your dead body over there. 'Tisn't

23

exactly convenient, is it, at this particular moment? Nobody isn't going to take you with all that lot."

He reflected for a moment, spat again – this time from the other side of his mouth, narrowly missing Loïc: now it was his turn to shudder.

"Right, now I'll tell you what I'll do. I'll take you back to the farm. And then tomorrow I'll see if I can find you another car. My mother'll see these ladies have somewhere to sleep, and as for the men, well, we'll see . . . Perhaps you could sleep in the barn. Right, let's go. Gid on."

He lifted the reins and the horses took a step forward. Loïc stepped back, hands in the air:

"Ah, wait. I'll have to go and explain things to the others."

The poor farmer had no idea what taking a decision entailed when it involved Diane and Luce, the one having such decided views, the other almost none, making one wonder which was the greater nuisance . . . not forgetting Bruno, who was a complete pain-in-the-neck. But Loïc, come what may, was going in the cart with the farmer; he being the only human still around with any common sense, he thought, as his gaze came to rest on the interminable jam stretching as far as the horizon. A farm. A farm with cold water, fresh hay, a real farm with horses, friendly dogs, that scent of green grass and earth he had not savoured since childhood – Deauville or Cannes did not have the same smell.

The young farmer was becoming a bit edgy.

"Do as you want, then. But I don't have much time to waste. We has to get the harvest in before the Bosch sets fire to it. We're lucky 'tis still

24

hot. Now if you're coming, you'll have to come right away."

"We're coming, we're coming. Many thanks," Loïc said.

And, instinctively, he held out his hand, introduced himself.

"Loïc Lhermitte."

"Maurice Henri."

They gravely shook hands, and Loïc ran towards his harem, which he found in mid-battle, because Bruno had the sulks.

"Listen, Diane, Luce: the farmer over there has suggested he take us back to his place to sleep for the night. Tomorrow he'll find us a car. I can't honestly see any alternative."

"Sleep with that bumpkin? Stand in dung up to our necks? No, Loïc, you're mad." Bruno's face was white, his teeth gritted: he was furious, the delayed fuse on his fear at last detonating.

"I'm no snob, but all the same. You obviously haven't a clue what French farms are like, that's for sure."

Loïc had a moment of giddiness or it could have been anger. His vision became blurred. He wanted to hit this smoothie, this gigolo.

"You've no idea what you're saying, Bruno. First of all, yes, you are a snob. Secondly, you know no more about French farms than I do, anyway. If we don't take up this offer, we'll have to sleep by the roadside tonight. Well, I'm going. As for the "bumpkin" who's offered a roof for the four of us, I personally find him most kind. So I'm going. What about you two women?"

25

"I'm going too," said Diane. "I've no intention of spending the night in this hellhole with petrol around and people who could rob us blind the moment it's dark. Oh, no thanks. I'm right behind you Loïc."

And, in anticipation of rustic misery, she took on a courageous, resigned attitude. Luce glanced at Bruno who turned his back on her, then at Loïc, before saying, to everyone's general amazement:

"You do what you like, Bruno, but I'm not going to leave poor Jean lying here on the ground with the ants. I'm going with them, and that's that."

"Then you know very well I'll have to come with you," Bruno hissed. "I can't leave you all alone at this farm, God knows what sort of people will be there . . . but you'll pay for it."

He must have been relieved to give duty as an excuse. The road was a nightmare in daytime as it was, let alone at night. With a shrug of his shoulders, Loïc took the lead of their little caravan.

"Don't forget the suitcases," he called back to Bruno.

Quite suddenly he felt like a man of authority, and determined, yes, determined his decisions be respected. Yet again, it was the first time such a thing had happened to him. For a very long time . . .

"But don't ask me to say anything to a man like that or shake hands with him," Bruno shouted into their backs. "It's not on."

"What the hell do I care what you do," Loïc said.

Walking quietly beside him, the two women nodded to each other in silent approval. Loïc was becoming more and more astonishing. And more and more entertaining, Diane thought.

"You does right to hurry, because by this time tomorrow, with this heat, your friend here won't be very fresh," the farmer said, thus, confirming his invitation with this gentle proposition.

The two women shuddered, obediently climbed on to the cart and sat next to the farmer, on the only seat. Jean was stretched along the slatted side of the cart at the front, Bruno and Loïc sat at the back with their four feet, like their spirits, dangling in the void, keeping a death-vigil.

An hour later, or two, or even three (Diane's watch had given up with all the shaking) and as their bucolic procession was crossing a plain similar to an incredible number of other mournful plains they had already crossed, the farmer, firmly wedged between Diane on his left flank and Luce on his right, stopped the horses, and pointing his whip towards the still empty horizon, broke the silence of the fields to announce: "We're here."

But there was nothing in front of his whip except fertile land, which, though it was under cultivation, still looked like a desert.

"I can't see anything," Diane said in her usual forthright way, while Luce, still feeling irresponsible and cowardly and huddled on her wooden seat with her head hunched into her shoulders, let out a small cry of anguished doubt. In the back, the two men broke off their contemplation of the cart tracks' swivelled round to face front, and stared worriedly into the distance, which was as empty for them as it had been for their companions.

While the four exchanged furtive, wary looks, the farmer gave a brief laugh.

"You can't see it from here. You can't see the farmhouse, but there's a coomb behind them trees."

Undoubtledly irritated by their mistrustful looks, he once more brandished his whip towards the distant horizon, and in so doing, as if by an optical illusion, seemed to awaken and release a final Stuka, until then invisible and inaudible, which now swooped down from above, insensitive to their rustic appearance.

"Oh no," Diane said, as it appeared and began to grow in size before their very eyes. "Oh no. This can't be true. It's not fair."

And a surge of anger swamped her fear. She shook her fist at the sky as the same clamour and clatter as before burst around them. Since they had left the road and cut across the fields, Diane, perched on her wooden seat, had gradually drifted into a state of mind which was of course very far from being happy, but not so far from being serene. And it was with a kind of horror and bitterness that she now found herself wrenched from the gentle rolling motion of the cart and jolted furiously from right to left and left to right. But since man is the only animal that can adjust to *any*thing, Diane could, while earth and sky changed places and her eardrums were bursting, establish some distinctive sounds amidst the pandemonium and abomination they were enduring. She recognized a man's cry, the farmer's, as well as a fresh bout of yelping from Luce, followed almost immediately, in the middle of this apocalypse, by the despairing, frantic, astonished neighing of the horses, who doubtless until then had been spared the echoes of war.

Hardly had this inferno moved away, than Diane's apparently intact mind sorted through the whole commotion and confirmed that the young farmer had just been wounded and had let the horses bolt. When the furious momentum which threw her first to the right towards the others, that is, the bleeding farmer slumped over Luce, and the no less furious momentum which brought her back again into her corner, that is, towards the left, and threw her – since there was nothing to stop her – into the void, her calculations proved correct both about this and the ensuing danger . . . for, immediately, she swayed outwards and saw the ground stream past under her bulging eyes at an inconceivable speed, even for someone who had often ridden in a Bugatti. Diane thought she was done for.

But, due to two completely trivial factors, she escaped death, an original form of death certainly, but disagreeable for a woman of her social standing: that of falling from a farm cart. First, her high heels had wedged in a bad join in the floorboards, and now held her there, thus preventing her two feet from following the rest of her body. Secondly, through some long, boring massages and some no less tedious physical exercises, practised by thousands of society women the world over, she unknowingly and almost against her better judgement had acquired some bulges under the flabby surface of her skin which could now, without flattery, qualify as muscles. These muscles enabled her to make a sort of desperate upward twist to her back, while she brushed against the handle of the handbrake,

29

a round, creaking, cast-iron handle which she gripped with all the strength she could muster in her fingers and her contracted body. Few women, few acrobats and few athletes would have achieved what Diane Lessing achieved that day, impromptu and under a blazing sun, and what's more, without the benefit of an audience. For her public had at that same moment been jumbled together and intertwined, pitched and tossed in all directions, without the least regard for their heroic female driver.

Once restored to the livng world, that is to say, to the back of the cart, half-kneeling and still shaking, Diane could think only of one thing: I'm alive. I'm alive again. And it's entirely due to me; it was an idea which had never remotely occurred to her before. Like many rich people, Diane had had a passive idea of her physiological fate. Her accidents were unfortunate circumstances due to exterior incompetence, her health a possession that fate was still trying to wrest from her, and her abilities a lost potential for sporting achievement. Her body had only ever been a place on which to burden her misery, never a source of pleasure.

And now, all at once, she owed her life to herself and through a kind of instinctive gratitude, decided to preserve it. It was the least she could do, she thought with sombre pride. And still shaken like a rag-doll, but holding firmly to the guardrail, she fumbled with her hand and managed to find the reins in the farmer's open, helpless hands.

She held on and slowly stood up in the cart.

It was many years ago that Parisian Society had said

– either in sarcasm or in fear – that Diane Lessing was capable of anything. This same Parisian Society would therefore have been astonished only by the setting of the demonstration, when they saw Diane Lessing standing astride the back of a farm cart, throwing into relief a profile uniquely her own, pulling on the reins of two bolting carthorses, and emitting wild cries, incomprehensible to the human ear, incomprehensible doubtless to the animals' too, since, when the horses finally came to a halt, not only were they sweating and trembling, their eyes bulging, their mouths flecked with foam – a manifestation of fear with animals – but their ears were bent forward and very wide apart: in a flagrant sign of curiosity. Whatever it was, they stopped, and Diane turned triumphantly to her unseeing and intertwined companions, both at the front and back of the cart, before asking what had happened to her handbag.

The farmer had been shot in the ankle, and after suggesting she make a tourniquet with her own scarf, Diane finally decided to use Luce's instead, since the wound was bleeding so much: the aforementioned scarf would inevitably be ruined. And so it was done. The farmer revived, resting against Luce's bosom and watered by Luce's tears, but as soon as the cart began to jolt, fell unconscious again. Even so, the young man had told the truth, for after a few more kilometres, the horses led them to the edge of a coomb, which had been invisible to the naked eye, but lay in the hollow of a field; and at the bottom, surrounded by trees, was the farm: a big L-shaped building, with an appearance every bit as rustic as they had all more or less feared.

Chapter 3

After she had cast a jaundiced eye over these drab buildings, Diane once more set the cart in motion. She separated the reins and clicked her tongue like a professional, then started to shout, "Boo! Boo! Boo!" which, for some reason Loïc could not pinpoint, set his teeth on edge rather than amused him, now that he'd joined her on the seat of command.

"It's not "Boo! boo!" he muttered, against his better judgement.

Having had her confidence boosted by her obedient steeds, Diane turned her exasperated face towards him:

"What's not what?"

"It's not 'Boo! boo!' you say to horses. But, honestly, it really doesn't matter, Diane. It's more important to pay attention to the track ahead."

Alas, he had touched a very new but also very raw nerve as far as Diane's pride was concerned.

"So, it's not 'Boo! boo!?" she asked in an astounded, sarcastic voice, which reminded Luce of occasions when she ranted, and she gave Loïc a frightened glance.

"Well then, my dear, if it's not too much to ask,

perhaps you'd be kind enough to tell me what it should be?"

Loïc struggled, already regretting his remark:

"I don't know, um, precisely. But I'd have thought it better to say: "Gee up, and whoa"." He smiled with even more embarrassment, since the silence within the coomb was twice as resonant as up above at field level.

"Gee up whoa?" Diane repeated, her eyes searching the surrounding bushes as if to quiz some agrarian god who might be lurking in them. "Gee up whoa?" she repeated incredulously. "Dear Loïc, are you sure? Does this stem from some personal recollection, or is it the fruit of your reading?"

"Oh, let's drop it," he said, turning away as he started to climb over to his peaceful place next to Bruno in the back of the cart, but a bump in the track forced him to hang on to the seat.

"Would you care to take the reins? You should've done it just now when the horses had the bit between their teeth and were heading at a gallop towards the next disaster. Your "Gee up whoa" would have stopped them in their tracks. It's idiotic that, in my ignorance, I didn't know of this phrase sooner. I could've avoided having to wrestle with these." (Diane indicated the reins in her hands.) "And I needn't have broken two of my fingernails when I was shouting "Boo". Just look though, these polite animals are pretending they know what I mean. Look, they've completely calmed down. All the same, if you don't mind' Loïc, I'd like to try out your "Gee up whoa" on them – if it's their proper lingo."

34

"Oh, Diane," Loïc said, now exhausted and irritated as well, for Bruno's face had a treacherously gleeful expression as he listened to their exchange. "Really, it's not worth it."

"It's always worth learning. Don't you think you two?" she cried to her faithful carthorses. "We'll try it. Let's do it. Gee up whoa, gee up whoa, gee up whoa," she shouted derisively, but in such a stentorian voice, that the (perhaps polyglot) horses were spurred into automatic acceleration – unless of course the real reason for their new lease of energy was the nearness of their stable.

As they cantered into the farmyard, Loïc felt more anxious than triumphant.

"Whoa, whoa."

The shades of some ancestral gentlemen-farmers whispered the right word to bring the animals to a halt; which coincided with the end of their discussion.

The buildings, as has been said, formed an L-shape, the first part being the dwelling-house, the second the farm buildings themselves, which were full of joyful activity. There was the combine-harvester, standing baroquely lopsided like some prehistoric beast. Geese honked somewhat threateningly, plonking their huge flat feet in the muck while the different mooings and bellowings stirred something in their childlike hearts. This animal restlessness, so close to the silent, sinister house, through whose half-closed shutters filtered neither voice nor sound, was disturbing, as was the great wooden door with its broken latch and the windows masked with tattered curtains.

"It's like *Des Adrets' Inn*," Loïc said, looking at

35

it, his sharp eyes, as always, wide with curiosity and amusement.

"Ah, what a remarkable protector to have in a world as backward and disconcerting as this," Diane thought. Bruno, on the other hand, had limited himself to opening his case and removing a beige roll-neck sweater which he put on, pulling it over his grim face. And, indeed, it was already becoming a little cooler. The sun had sunk low in the sky, and was now half hidden by the wan grey fields, those interminable fields above.

"Des Adrets' Inn?" Luce asked. "Where's that? the inn I mean? I'd absolutely love to freshen up my make-up properly."

"Soon Luce, but not at "Des Adrets". The inn was famous for bumping off its customers after dinner."

"That's all we'd need," Diane cried, driven to her limits. "Don't you think we've had enough incidents for one day? Do we have to have our throats slit in the night now by a bunch of peasants. Thank you, thank you so much."

"You're not thinking of sleeping here, are you?" Bruno turned to them disgustedly.

"And where would you like to sleep?" Loïc was leaning against the cart, his hands in his pockets, his linen jacket all crumpled and his tie loose, and he suddenly looked virile – it suited him.

There was a second's hesitation while they all looked at each other and turned to the young farmer, who was practically lying on top of Luce and still bleeding. The scarf was soaked now. A complete write-off," Diane thought, and was quite proud of her foresight.

"But I can't truly believe," she said, "that this young man hasn't anyone to cook for him or talk to him? What's going to become of us? We've already got a dead body and now we've got a wounded one as well." She had launched into a painful and bitter recitative when she was interrupted by the arrival of a thin woman clad in black, with an austere, grim face who, having glanced at them without apparent surprise, climbed on to the step of the cart, seized the semi-conscious youth around the waist and proceeded to haul him out. Loïc and Diane rushed forward quite mechanically and helped her remove the unconscious boy. They even started carrying him into the house, with Loïc holding his shoulders and Diane his feet, obeying the woman in black's imperious beckoning. But after a couple of paces, Diane stopped, swaying on her feet.

"I can't . . . I really can't do any more, Loïc. I'm going to collapse. I just can't carry him. I can't do another thing. I'm clapped out. What is it you want? There are moments in life . . ."

And cold-bloodedly she let the boy's feet fall to the ground and went to sit on the step to empty her heart out.

"I don't know if you've totted it up, Loïc, but since this morning we've been machine-gunned three or four times, our chauffeur's been killed in front of us, our car demolished and gone up in flames, our host's been shot through the ankle with a bullet, his horses have bolted, and it's a miracle I could control them . . . and now here we are in some farmyard begging sanctuary from a woman who can't speak a word of French. It's not

37

much use having nerves of steel. I'm telling you, Loïc, mine're disintegrating."

"You're quite right, Diane, but even so, we can't just leave this poor boy lying on the ground. We've still got to do something."

Like a snake, Diane whipped round to face Bruno, who, quite unruffled, was still trying on pullovers, and only two paces away from poor Jean.

"Bruno," she screeched. "Bruno, come and help us."

"I've already told you. I'm not lifting a finger for those bumpkins."

After a silence which was too marked not to be offensive, Diane's voice rent the air like a trumpet or a clarion call, or like a martial instrument at any rate.

"I'm warning you, Bruno: if you don't help Loïc this instant, when we get back to Paris, or to New York, I'll tell the saga of your cheque to everyone who's anybody: your famous cheque . . . that American woman's cheque . . . you know the one."

Bruno took two steps forward, his face pale, his voice high-pitched like an adolescent's."

"You wouldn't do that, Diane, you couldn't. Even you would look ridiculous."

"Ridicule won't kill me at my age, my friend . . . at my age people show sympathy. But it's lethal at yours. You'd be finished. You'd be a social outcast. I'd see to it personally. Believe me."

Without more ado, Bruno stepped forward, took the farmer by the legs and lifted him up to carry him into the house. They found themselves in a big dark room, where at first they could see nothing except the woman who was impatiently beckoning them to an alcove bed in the wall, covered with old blankets. There they lay the wounded man before making for the door. All they had time to glimpse in this room was the glow of a huge fire, despite the torrid heat outside. The room was clearly what Diane would have called the "living room", if she could have ventured to use such a fashionable English word there without sounding comical even for a moment. Even so, neither of them had paid any attention to the décor: Bruno through deliberate obtuseness, and Loïc, because his mind was on other matters: he was already intrigued by this story of the American cheque, which had whetted his appetite for social gossip. He would not be content until Diane had told him everything.

Somewhat revived, Diane now majestically entered the room. Once inside she stopped and stretched her neck like a heron, her eyes swivelling comically in their sockets. With her crumpled costume, untidy make-up and dishevelled hair, she looked like some antique-dealer ·who'd spent a fruitless afternoon looking for furniture, or a charity lady who'd done the same for orphans. Quite suddenly the distinguished, elegant Diane Lessing had all the appearance of a grumpy shopkeeper, Loïc thought.

And, miraculously, she at last discovered a significance in their travels. Strutting like a bantam, her eyes glittering with an excitement which none of the dreadful moments of the day had managed to quell, she clung to Loïc's arm and said in an imperious whisper.

"Loïc, just look at that table. It's exactly what I was looking for for Zizi Maple. And the bread bin. How wonderfully chic! And what about that grandfather clock over there, simply marvellous isn't it? D'you think they'd sell it to us? What a pity no one can take advantage of this beautiful furniture. Oh, I'm absolutely potty about that clock."

"We can hardly take the clock to the States," Loïc said, being practical for once. "Perhaps it might be better to wait till the war's over."

"Oh, it's so peaceful here. It's really good," Luce said. "I had one of my panic attacks just now. I keep having panic attacks today."

"So did the horses," Diane remarked. "I honestly don't know how I managed to stop them."

"Oh, Diane. You were wonderful," Luce said with genuine enthusiasm that brought a lump to Diane's throat.

Loïc smiled at her.

"Alas, I didn't see a thing. I was hanging out of the cart, clinging on to some bit of rail for dear life, and squirming like a lunatic trying to get back in. So was Bruno, weren't you?"

But Bruno, who was looking contemptuously round the room, shrugged his shoulders and did not reply.

"What's the story of the American cheque?" Loïc whispered to Diane, who whispered back:

"I'll tell you one of these days . . . if you're good. Let's see to our hosts first."

She walked resolutely across to the alcove where the woman was sitting with the boy and dressing his foot with some strange compresses, that looked as though they had an earth base with some blackish gauze.

"Is he a little better? The wound looks so horrible.

40

You know, the dear boy got that through helping us?"

Then, as the farmer's wife neither looked up nor at her, Diane decided to open fire.

"My name's Diane Lessing," she said, extending her hand right under the woman's nose, who, taken by surprise, shook it.

". . . and this is Loïc Lhermitte, Luce Ader and Bruno Delors. We're truly sorry to invade you like this, my dear Madame. We do apologize. But" – and she pointed to Maurice – "without him, we'd all be dead. Like our poor Jean . . ." she added. "My God", she cried standing on tiptoe and beating the air with her arms. "My God, we'd forgotten him. Is he still in the cart?"

"He can hardly come to harm out there, now he's dead, can he?" Bruno said dryly, at the same time reluctantly shaking the woman's hand like everyone else; while she, though visibly disconcerted, let them do it, with no sign of curiosity, but no hostility either.

"Arlette," she said. "Arlette Henri. And this here's my son Maurice. And over there's Granfer," she said, pointing to an armchair near the fire, towards which they all turned but could see nothing but an old blanket.

"Are you ladies and gentlemen thirsty?" Arlette asked. Arlette, the name of a woman of easy virtue, seemed singularly inept, for her face closely resembled something out of a Memling painting, thought Diane. For in her world, austere faces were always like something out of a Memling painting, just as pretty women were like Botticellis, scenes of horror like something

41

out of Bosch, banquets and snow Brueghel, fat women Renoir, thin women Modigliani, while the inspired but unfortunate concatenation of an ear, a bridge and a chair was how she thought of Van Gogh . . .

The four travellers vigorously nodded assent. They had drunk nothing for some hours, in spite of emotions and sun – the one as intense as the other.

"I could drink a small bottle of anything."

Diane had decided to adopt a language which rose to the occasion, as Loïc remarked with trepidation.

"There's some Pastis, or homemade Plum, or red wine of course," Arlette enthused. And took several glasses and three unlabelled bottles from the sideboard.

"Have you nothing non-alcoholic?" Diane simpered. "With this heat. Oh well, never mind. After all we've been through, I think I'll have some homemade Plum . . . it's probably the most wholesome . . ."

"I think I'll try some red wine, with a little water," Loïc said. He signalled to Luce to do the same.

"Small and neat, eh?"

Diane laughed. She raised her glass, raised her eyebrows when she saw the meagre contents, and with a condescending chuckle downed the splendid homemade Plum in one gulp. A moment later she was coughing, spitting and tottering on her square-heeled sports shoes, rapidly encircling the table, her two arms stretched in front of her and her eyes closed like a medium in mid-trance. Loïc intercepted her just as she finished her first lap of the table and was about to embark on her second, and forced her to sit down.

"It be a bit strong," Arlette conceded.

While Diane's cough was abating, Loïc asked for news of the wounded.

"How are you treating the wound? Have you called a doctor?"

"We don't have no telephone here. I put a bit of Plum on it to disinfect it, and some iodine, and then a cobweb with some pyretic earth on it – I always has some put by, in the house. The bullet haven't touched the bone, it went right through, so . . ."

"Cobwebs? Real cobwebs?"

Luce seemed truly concerned about her host. Bruno peevishly lit a cigarette and exhaled the smoke, in the manner of Al Capone.

"And that cleans it?" Luce went on. She sounded surprised.

"He's still alive isn't he?" his mother said with exasperated logic. "And what's more, I can tell you, ever since this young man were a little boy, he've spent all his time falling over and hurting himself on every possible thing that can cut. 'Tis a wonder he haven't done it today with all the harvesting. 'Tis just the sort of time he do it. Can you imagine what 'tis like with the harvesting going on?"

Diane who, having dried her eyes, was now blowing her nose and catching her breath, leant under the table to get her handbag, but swiftly withdrew in order to speak to the mistress of the house:

"My God, Arlette, a hen has just come in. Look!" And indeed a chicken flew up from under the table, then pattered across the floor. But Arlette/Memling looked at Diane blankly, and quite unmoved when two other very busy fowl emerged from the next room, cackling. Diane's face lost its sympathetic aura and became reproving.

"I think we've entered Cro-Magnon territory," she said to Loïc.

Loïc, who had hardly recovered from his urge to laugh a moment before, fought against the current bout now threatening to erupt. Things were made worse by Luce showing a great interest in the poultry: Diane's and Arlette's contradictory reactions must have troubled her great inner calm, and she was obviously weighing the pros and cons of these chickens. Perhaps she might even want to take advantage of their presence to formulate a personal opinion, Loïc thought. A lump mounted and receded in his throat, obliging him to retreat into the background, eyes half-closed and evasive, his voice stifled.

"I'm going to give you soup and cheese," Arlette said. "And perhaps some eggs, If, that is, those sluts has laid them," she added to general surprise.

The Parisians looked hard at her, with the same apologetic numbness that the Prime Minister had induced in his own ministers when he'd described them as "clots". And all three raised their lowered eyes with those impassive expressions which follow a gaff or impropriety in conversation. That finished Loïc. He was now in a trance with head down, hands clasped to the chair rail; about to explode a hundred metres into the air, in his effort not to succumb to laughter.

"It's a long time since I've eaten soup," Luce remarked melancholically – and unexpectedly for her too – so Diane said soothingly:

"It's exactly the same as what we call a *potage*,

but probably not so velvety," she said reassuringly.

At this point Loïc tiptoed from the room, bent double, muttering inaudible excuses.

"It's his nerves." "A delayed reaction." "Whatever's the matter with him?" . . . "Some fresh air will do him good . . . a little time on his own . . ."

This last prediction was the only incorrect one, for there on the cart Loïc rediscovered poor Jean's corpse, which they had forgotten and which, to his shame, could not immediately stop him laughing. Eventually he calmed down, and returned to the room.

"You've forgotten poor Jean on the cart . . ."

Moved by a sense of duty, and uttering cries of indignation and remorse, the two women rose, and almost as quickly sat down again, not knowing how to accomplish it.

"Best put him in the cellar," said the wounded man who had now awoken. "My mother'll show you the way."

"I'll go with her to tie up the horses." Her role of horsewoman had turned Diane into a person of responsibility.

"No need, they're as gentle as lambs," said Madame Memling, looking tired as she directed them towards the door, followed by Loïc.

Bruno took advantage of Loïc's absence to lecture Luce.

"Don't you think, dear, we'd do better to find a town, and a post office and wire your husband about the delay and look for some transport to get us to Lisbon?"

"It *would* be a good idea," Diane said, even before

Luce could open her mouth, "if *you* went, it would be a very good idea. You're a man, aren't you? We're actually extremely tired ourselves."

"I was talking to Luce."

"And I'm replying on Luce's behalf."

They confronted each other.

"If we don't know anyone else around here," Luce said determinedly just for once, "we're not going to start walking somewhere in the dark. And quite honestly I'm too tired to get into that ramshackle cart again."

She had a scared, plaintive expression which her lover found reassuring, and irritated Diane even more.

"I can't wait for the soup," she said. "And then bed."

"Loïc and I'll be consigned to the barn I should imagine."

"Well, don't take advantage of the situation to lead Loïc astray, Bruno," Diane said, but no one appreciated the quip.

Loïc and Arlette were already back, apparently unaffected, and Loïc left again with three candles, offered majestically by the mistress of the house so that the poor corpse could have some light.

"I'll take first watch," Luce said with emotion. But as soon as she had drunk her soup, and eaten her cheese and egg, she tottered off with Diane to an empty room, occupied by a huge thronelike bed, which scarcely had they made, than they fell into it. And with a crucifix at their head, and a pitcher at their side, they immediately fell asleep.

The men also had a room and a bed, despite Bruno's predictions.

Loïc put the mattress on the floor and lay on it, leaving the bed-base to Bruno – who had suddenly become prudish now that he came to undress – not realizing that Loïc would far rather have punched him on the jaw than kissed him.

Why do they think homosexuals behave like that? he wondered vaguely before closing his eyes. As if they devoted all their time trying to seduce their fellow men. What narcissism. How hypocritical humans were. It was his last thought before he fell asleep.

Chapter 4

To city-dwellers like these, a cock-crow always signalled it was time to wake up: like the noise of dustbins in town – a graceless clatter, however talented the dustman was, but having more charm than the tireless, relentless vocalizing of this creature. Nineteenth-century tales in the Dickens' genre, with wayfaring heroes who yearned to strangle the cock at dawn, now seemed far less exaggerated.

Loïc held his silence and kept his eyes closed, in order not to have to endure Bruno's vituperations from his elevated position on the bed-base. Luce on the other hand, lying next to snoring Diane, wondered anguishedly where she was as she opened her eyes. A pain in her side like cramp reminded her of her appendix operation and of her three faithful friends who, because of her, had had to put up with the crowing cock. Tears of gratitude, then remorse, flooded her eyes . . . even Bruno, who was so disagreeable, had waited for her. She decided she would take them breakfast in bed, envisaging herself in a white pinafore with a tray of toast. Noiselessly she slipped out of bed, opened her suitcase which had been thrown into the room, and forgetting her maidly role, took out her beach clothes: a pair of straw-coloured, low-waisted slacks, a raw silk shirt with a plaited leather Hermès belt, and open sandals which would leave her feet free. She ran the comb through her hair, put on only light make-up (which suited her), and then stepped out into a dark corridor, abandoning Diane who was still snoring her regular dry snore, without the variations which can be torture.

Dear Diane. So energetic, so devoted throughout all their difficulties. And dear Bruno as well, despite his contempt for the handsome farmer, he'd been willing to help, and kind in bringing him into the house. Loïs had been marvellous . . . Everything was going well. All she had to do was hide her attraction to the farmer from Bruno. But it was going to be difficult, for she had awoken feeling the same way she'd felt on going to bed: totally infatuated.

When they'd been sitting side by side on the cart, she'd thought she would go off her head every time he brushed against her. The plane had attacked them just in time. Then the ensuing panic and the young man being wounded afterwards had prevented her betraying her feelings to the others. He, on the other hand, had understood them very well she recalled, and blushed: she stumbled in the corridor at the memory of that calloused hand placed on her right thigh.

The mother was already in the yard. She was calling "Come on, come on, my little ones," in her harsh voice. With an air of innocence, Luce walked towards the voice but couldn't resist passing the alcove where she was not surprised to feel herself grabbed by Maurice (Maurice? Or Henri?). In the semi-darkness framed by the open door on to the yard and the little shutter above the kitchen range, she could vaguely see the young man sitting on the bed, bare-chested, and smiling at her with his big white teeth.

"Maurice?" she said.

"Yes, come and sit here a moment."

Luce obeyed, her legs trembling.

Even had he not asked her, she would still have lain beside him. How shameless for someone who was André Ader's wife, Bruno Delors' mistress, but how exciting as well!

"Are you in pain?" she asked.

She put her hand on his wounded ankle. Maurice took it and held it tightly in his own.

"I'd like to go with you," he said.

The term "to go", although quite new to Luce, did not remain obscure for long.

"'Tis all because of you, I brought back that bunch of crackpots in my cart," he said laughing. "You do have some funny friends."

"They're very kind," Luce said, but a feeling of concern stopped her.

She couldn't imagine herself in this alcove, exposed to every draught and every passer-by in the house – let alone the hens. Maurice forestalled her.

"I'll get up just now, I'll use a stick and we'll find a place, you'll see. The farm's big and there's hay everywhere. 'Tisn't that bothering me. No, 'tis the harvesting, you know, 'tis about the harvesting I'm thinking. The wheat's got to be cut right away, now, in June, before the Fritz gets to it and sets fire to it and destroys it."

Luce gazed at him tenderly, overcome that her new lover should be more concerned about the harvest than her. She had always liked serious men: Bruno's indolence and inactivity were what she reproached him most for . . . And apropos of him, how was she going to manage "to go" with Maurice? What about Bruno? And Loïc? and Diane? And also, surely, they'd be leaving again during the course of the day? The idea of leaving this man without getting to know him (in the biblical sense) seemed frightfully unjust to her.

"What if we leave?" she said, squeezing the boy's hand.

"And how d'you think you'll do that? There's a pickup here, but the engine don't go no more. The mechanic at Silbert's supposed to be coming out, but you can imagine with all those cars on the road, he'll be making his packet as it is. You won't be leaving on horseback will you? Anyway, your friends should give me a hand with the harvesting. I can't do nothing in this state," he said despairingly.

And Luce, who was looking at him rather than listening, nevertheless heard the note of affliction in his voice and kissed his hand. She felt secure and confident with this stranger, as with no other man before.

"You're terrible pretty," he said in a childlike voice.

Luce's face lit up. It had been a very long time since anyone had mentioned she was beautiful to her face. In Paris, it wasn't done, and she missed it.

It was then that they heard a harsh, ear-splitting bray coming from the back of the room; it was so strident that Luce shot up and in one bound was two paces from the alcove.

"Ghee-maw, ghee-maw," it bellowed.

"'Tis all right. 'Tis only Granfer."

He laughed. He couldn't see how atrocious the cry sounded. And the fact that it belonged to an invisible old man made it even more atrocious.

"He's saying 'Good morning'," Maurice explained, "only as he hasn't got no teeth, it sound like 'Ghee-maw'. You better answer him, eh, otherwise he'll get angry."

"Good morning, sir," Luce replied in a trembly voice, and Maurice doubled up with laughter.

She was amazed that her companions had not come rushing into the room, appalled by this voice from another world, from another species even, where mad people were free to roam at will and given the place of honour in an armchair by the fire.

"I didn't see him yesterday?" she said.

"Well, he was here when we arrived. But you can't see him by the fire because he's so thin. My mother attended to him before the meal so we could eat in peace."

"Oh, it's no joke growing old," Luce murmured, terrified but sincere.

All at once she felt a little less attracted to Maurice. Not that she specially believed in heredity, but the idea that he could tolerate having such a horror so close to him alarmed her about the rest of the farm. She might just be unlucky enough to walk into a three-footed sheep or a two-headed horse, or God knows what abomination. Of course, it was not poor Maurice's fault . . . he – one had to admit – seemed very normal.

"And how long has monsieur, your grandfather, sorry, been like he is?"

53

"Well, ages. He's talked like that since the day he lost all his teeth. His mind isn't all there neither."

"How could he have lost all his teeth in one go? What symptoms did he have?"

"He didn't have no symptoms. He was mending the barn and a beam fell on his head. Hasn't moved for fifteen years now, he just calls out . . . But you gets used to it. He isn't my mother's father, he's my father's father."

"You still have a father? You're lucky."

"Yes," Maurice seemed unsure. "My father's at the front. He was taken prisoner first, and my brother three days later," he announced with a sort of pride. "But 'tis bad luck for the harvesting, 'tis what's so annoying . . . As my mother says: 'tis less work in the kitchen and less work in the fields. I'm hoping the Faberts, our neighbours, is coming to give us a hand, and now your friends is here, perhaps things'll go better."

Could it be that this handsome man was banking on Loïc and Bruno to help with the harvest? He was a bit wide of the mark. After all the emotion of the morning, Luce let out a sort of nervous laugh, and to hide it, she turned to Maurice and lay her head against his shoulder, which smelt good – of man and hay . . .

"Ghee-maw, ghee-maw," the horrible old man brayed again and she leapt up.

Which was just as well, for at that moment Diane appeared in the room, wearing a leafy-patterned dressing gown.

"Ah Luce, did you sleep well? When I think that all

morning long we've had to endure that dreadful cock. And now I can't work out what animal it is that's braying, really close by somewhere. It's unbearable. Whatever sort of beast can it be?"

She saw Maurice in his alcove and took note of the distance separating him from Luce, then began sniffing inquisitively.

"Good morning, dear Maurice. Have you slept well in spite of your wound? I have to confess that the silence of the countryside at first prevented sleep, and afterwards it was quite the reverse that awoke me. That cock, what an organ it must have for a voicebox. And after the cock, what on earth was it? You must know. You live here. That cry is terrifying, terrifying. I thought I was back in medieval times with the . . . the dinosaurs. No, that was before, wasn't it? But in any case, it sounded like a wild animal. For all I know, of course," she added prudently and with modesty.

She also laughed nervously. Luce hoped that she would come over to join them soon enough not to be too near the old man when he started braying again.

Luckily, in fact, Diane did come over just before the braying recommenced.

"Oh," Diane screamed in horror. "Oh, what is it? I could've sworn it came from this room, it sounds so close. I could swear it's not a domesticated animal."

Maurice laughed so loud that Luce herself had to explain, with her customary clarity.

"It's Monsieur Henri, the grandfather, I mean the father of his father, Maurice's grandfather in fact."

Diane, quite ashen, her hand still on her heart, looked at her severely.

"Yes? Good. Fine. But I didn't ask for the genealogy of the Henri family Luce. I merely asked you what made that dreadful noise?"

"But that's what I'm saying, it's his grandfather. It's he who . . . He lost all his teeth in a single day, with no symptoms."

"What symptoms? What's the connexion?"

"Well, he'd like to say 'Good morning', can't you see, Diane? And as he has no teeth, he can only say 'Ghee-maw' to you. That's the explanation."

"What ghee-maw? What are you reciting with your ghee-maws? I'm talking about . . ."

At that moment the grandfather, doubtless stimulated by all these unknown voices, let out another war cry and Diane leapt instinctively closer to the alcove, as if in search of human contact.

"You mean it's . . . it's him?" she stammered (for once). "It's him making that noise? But it's completely insane. How old is he?"

"It's not a question of age, Diane," Luce ventured to say. "It's a question of teeth you know . . . Because . . ."

"Tell me, you, young man, can you confirm that it's your grandfather making those inhuman cries?"

Diane turned to Maurice and looked him straight in the eye as if challenging him to tell the truth.

"Well yes, 'tis him," said Maurice, suddenly unhappy. "'Tis him. If he's disturbing you, you tell me what I can do. He's been doing it for the last fifteen years. You'll have to get used to it, that's all."

Diane wavered a little under the leaves of her dressing gown. She looked like the pattern on it of an exotic squawking bird. She took two steps and sank into a chair a good distance from the invalid.

"Doubtless one can get used to anything," she murmured dreamily, drumming her varnished nails on the rustic table (object of the previous day's desires). "Surely one can adjust to anything," she repeated two or three times, just as if she were going gaga, Luce thought anxiously.

But Diane shook herself and began to recover her composure, when Maurice, either out of irritation or sadism, called her to order.

"You must say 'Good morning' as well you know. Otherwise he gets angry. You must answer him."

"Because he has to be answered? Wonderful. What am I supposed to say? Ghee-maw, Ghee-maw? Me as well?" (Diane had adopted the patient voice of a great lady.)

"No no, you don't have to go to no trouble. You got teeth, haven't you?"

"Well, it's true I do have a few left," she conceded icily.

"Well then, you can say 'Good morning' to him properly."

Diane hesitated. She looked at him, looked at Luce, then turned towards the shadows and called out:

"Good morning sir, good morning," in a rather snobbish but polite, indeed cordial, voice.

To Luce's great relief, Loïc appeared in the doorway, his hair in his eyes. Very charming, I must say, Diane thought in her confused mind. Sweet, even for a homosexual in his fifties.

"Good morning all," Loïc cried, imprudently.

For immediately, as if challenged by that Good Morning, the old man bellowed a welcoming bray to Loïc, who, being pretty close, jumped, his eyes wild with alarm.

"What on earth was that?" he murmured. "Whatever was it? Whatever was it?" he repeated, casting imploring looks at his female friends and on this handsome, quite naked boy lying in bed over there, a trivial detail compared with the walking terror.

"It's the grandfather," Diane cried to him across the room. "I swear Loïc, it's the grandfather braying like that. As I said, Loïc, Cro-Magnon. We've entered Cro-Magnon territory."

"Shush," Luce rolled her bulging eyes, her finger to her lips.

"Have you heard of the Cro-Magnons, Monsieur Henri?" Diane calmly asked the wounded boy, who was beaming. He shook his head.

"You see, Luce. It makes no odds, we're almost part of the family in a manner of speaking. But what a performance. It's like a horror film. If I'd known about it yesterday, I'd never have closed my eyes. Just imagine if he'd started braying in the middle of the night? Oh . . . I've had the countryside up to here. I'm telling you, I can't take any more."

"As always, Diane, you exaggerate," Loïc said testily.

He too had blenched under the rain of ghee-maws and was trying dispiritedly to comfort his troupe, when an idea suddenly restored his aplomb.

"Has Bruno said 'Good morning' to our monsieur?"

"No, not yet. Yes, I hadn't thought of that."

58

And Diane also began to smile mollifyingly, almost happily.

Luce was wondering why, but without conviction, for the boy's hand under the sheet had found her leg and was fondling it nonchalantly through the coarse fabric of her slacks.

"Loïc, you know you must take your turn to say 'Good morning' to him."

Diane was jubilant as she watched Loïc, but he'd seen worse at the Quai d'Orsay and didn't turn a hair, simply raised his voice.

"Good day to you, monsieur. A very good day." At this juncture Arlette Memling arrived, carrying a bucket, brimful of milk, probably straight from the cow: milk that was so white, so frothy and so raw that Loïc felt instantly sick. Some tea. Quickly. His eyes revealed the first truly irritating and unfunny vexation this trip had had. He couldn't help his dejection, for he was always more prepared to put up with unhappiness that with vexations.

But that was because he had not taken Diane into account; she always brought tea with her on her travels. While Luce and Maurice, with the courage of youth, drank milk with barely a hint of coffee, he and Diane drank smoky tea, which in spite of the accompanying hunk of coarse bread, reminded their tastebuds of all the delights and refinements of Paris. Seeing Diane and Loïc in their dressing gowns, Luce in her beachwear, the half-naked boy, then the farmer's wife in her black smock, any census-taker would have compiled an extremely bizarre picture of France's rural population. Bruno was still asleep, it seemed, and no one taking part in the conversation missed him.

"The neighbour's little boy came by on his bicycle this morning," Arlette stated coldly. "Seems the Boche caught a packet at Tours and they're fighting all over the country. You mustn't leave your own home, 'tis dangerous, even round here. 'Tis all a terrible shambles and not a drop of petrol nowhere. I don't know how you're going to get away, you poor souls."

"It's unbelievable," Loïc said. "The Germans, with their tanks, fighting in Tours. It's totally unexpected, but it's fantastic."

"'Tis even more fantastic for 'tisn't only at Tours, 'tis the same in the north, so they say."

Loïc smiled happily, as did Diane and Luce. This resistance was of course totally unexpected and unhoped for, and perhaps it would last only a short while, but anything was better than long relentless retreat, this headlong flight all over France which depressed him so. At least they were fighting somewhere. At least the Germans understood that it was not open territory they were invading.

"As I understand it, we won't be able to leave," Diane said.

"That's it. You don't have no choice no longer," the mother cut in.

"But we're going to be a burden to you," Loïc protested.

"Don't worry about it," Madame Memling said categorically.

And they say peasants are unfriendly in France, Diane thought. How wrong they are.

60

"Don't think for one moment that we won't compensate you for our intrusion and for our bed and board, Madame," Loïc continued. "Consider us as paying guests, it's only fair."

"There's no question of it," Madame Memling declared severely. "No one pays money in our house, but you can pay in kind instead."

"Oh, pay in kind," Luce enthused, but some forbidden thoughts must have entered her mind for she stopped short and blushed.

The peasant woman's voice became firm.

"There's something though you should be worried about – 'tis your friend."

"What d'you mean, our friend?"

"'Tisn't going to help your friend with all this heat you understand. We've had losses like that on the farm in the summer, and you has to have the funeral quick, and that's the truth. 'Tis just that . . . the heat doesn't help neither the quick nor the dead." And seeing the others' horrified expressions, she added: "Your friend in the cellar I mean."

"Poor Jean," Luce said, recovering her spirits. "Is he still down there?"

"'Tis more than likely he's still down there, poor soul, and we'll shortly be smelling him up here."

In unison the two women took out their handkerchiefs and buried their faces in them.

"Well, look then," Maurice said annoyed. "We men can sort it out between us . . ."

And he tugged Loïc's arm, who was flattered that he had made absolutely no mention of Bruno when he'd uttered the words "we men".

"Can't help you myself. I'm really sorry about that. But I'll show you where the tools is and how to use them. Perhaps you should wake your friend now to give you a hand."

It was Luce who took upon herself this mission but who returned in tears ten minutes later to announce that Bruno, in accordance with the truce, he said, was refusing any task of this kind.

"Our young friend, who's also an ungracious bastard, has mad a pact to the effect that he won't lift a finger at the present moment," Loïc said to clarify the situation.

"He didn't make no pact with my mother," Maurice Henri laughed.

While they waited, it was Loïc who dug the grave in the meadow behind the house, a tomb under the apple trees which protected Loïc from the sun and would later protect poor Jean. A poetic spot with the four apple trees like four flowering candles, a spot he would gladly have chosen for his own carcass were he to have been digging his own grave. Bruno, decidedly, was a real little bastard. According to Maurice the ground was soft in this particular place and after Maurice's instructions Loïc now knew how to use a spade, but it still took him two hours to clear a big enough hole.

When he returned to the house he found Luce and Madame Memling seated in their chairs, looking serious and sombrely dressed, ready and waiting. It was eleven a.m. and while Loïc had been digging, the farmer's wife had taken the trouble to put some flowers on the dead man's chest, and place a crucifix made from two sticks and tied with a beautiful black ribbon in his hands. This

62

most pitiful extravagance together with the attempt at aesthetics combined to make the funeral preparations all the more poignant. Luce, in her costume of navy-blue, began to cry copiously. It was then that Diane made her entry into the kitchen, dressed all in black in a costume by Chanel, her face hidden under an unreal mantilla, and wearing the highest heels Loïc had ever seen. Her funeral outfit apparently had not dampened her morale.

"That's enough tears, Luce. After all, he was only . . ." She jammed on the brakes before saying "a chauffeur" and substituted "someone you hardly knew, after all".

"He worked for us for five years," Luce moaned. "I used to see him every day, we had such nice conversations when we were alone in the car."

"Nevertheless' you weren't on intimate terms," Diane said. Leaving the Henri family to wonder how one could not be on intimate terms with someone one had had nice conversations with every day for five years in the back of a car, she added firmly: "Isn't Bruno coming? Well, I'm going to say something to you Luce: with a creature like that, I wouldn't wait for someone to shoot him, I'd leave him on the spot."

But she was addressing Loïc when she said it, as if Luce was too much of a coward to understand her.

Jean had been laid out on the cart with the few flowers, by the farmer's wife and her son. Maurice was managing the horse, and the three women began walking behind, followed two paces further back by Loïc. His throat tightened when Luce began to cry twice as vehemently as before. How stupid, how horribly stupid this absurd death was of this man, on a road, with, and because of, people for whom he was a piece of furniture, and an unsigned piece at that.

The cart began its slow progress through the meadow, with Diane following all the more energetically, since she was pulling Luce by the arm. She took a huge stride, then two more and stopped dead, standing there, motionless, in the posture of a sportswomen: the allegory of a walker, but in marble. For her high heels had stuck in the pasty ground and stayed there as solidly as the pillars of the palaces of Venice in the lagoon. Simultaneously, Luce, who had taken a hurried step forward, was restrained brusquely by the elbow, and had to thrash around with both arms to keep her balance, and would have fallen on her behind had not Madame Memling caught her in flight. She turned to Diane. With her head held high and a distant look in her eye, Diane resembled Lot's wife turned to stone after Sodom and Gomorrah. All this time, unaware of the drama, Maurice and his horse continued on their way. Diane threw Loïc a bossy, desperate look.

"Why bury the poor devil in quick sands?" she hissed. "Are you so idle? Help me then."

Loïc tried vaguely to help her out by the waist – his conviction weakening the more an uncontrollable urge to laugh took over – the opposite of Luce, who was watching the disappearing cart and beginning to cry again. Not only had they killed her chauffeur, but his remains were now being hijacked.

Madame Memling barked at Diane: "Take your shoes off and walk in your socks."

It was a solution of course, although Diane did not much care for her stockings being referred to as "socks".

But she complied and they soon caught up with the cart, which had stopped by the hole dug with such difficulty by Loïc, the sight of which filled him with pride.

"I hope it's going to be big enough," he half-whispered. "I only had two hours to dig it in," he added to highlight his effort.

"But it's perfect, perfect," Diane said in a tone one would use to an obsequious gravedigger. "So are you going to get him down now?"

Loïc felt furious but tried to stay calm.

"Yes, but you've got to help me. I can't do it all on my own, Diane."

They were both whispering, aggressively, pettily, uselessly, Loïc thought with embarrassment.

"I'll give a hand," the farmer's wife offered. "I can see you isn't used to this sort of thing."

And with Loïc and Diane holding the shoulders and the farmer's wife the legs, they managed to slide Jean's corpse off the cart and lay it as gently as possible in the bottom of the pit. Then, panting and sweating, they stood in line: it took a good minute for them to regain the composure and grief-strickon manner required for the occasion. It was Diane, of course, who broke the silence first.

"We have to say something," she whispered to Loïc, "a blessing."

"Was he Christian?"

"I don't know," Luce said in a trembling voice.

"Well, so much for someone who spoke to him every day," Diane commented ironically.

Luce's voice rose two octaves: "We didn't talk about religion, don't you see?"

"I've no wish to hear what you talked about," Diane protested, being falsely discreet and lowering her eyes.

Loïc's irritation was beginning to mount.

"Does anyone know a burial prayer?"

Everyone shook their heads and Loïc took a deep breath.

Changing his voice in spite of himself, he began:

"Right. We are burying here our friend and brother Jean . . . Jean who?"

"I never could remember his surname," Luce said in a small shameful voice, but Diane, who was just opening her mouth, shut it again when she saw how meaningful and threatening a look Loïc was giving her.

". . . our brother Jean who died with us and for us on our journey. We consign him to the earth and to God . . . if he exists . . . and – " he checked himself quickly, ". . . if of course Jean believed he existed . . . We know nothing about him, nor about those who knew and loved him. Therefore," he said, making a mechanical sign of the cross to compensate for the sprinkling of atheism in his homily, "therefore we commend him into your care. And that's it. Amen."

"Amen," all the others repeated with relief.

He took some earth in his hand and let it fall on the white sheet, before turning away, bitter and saddened. And amused as well – he could no longer gauge his feelings. He waited for the others to copy him and move off with the cart. He waited until they had all left him, alone with this poor dead body, so that he could cover it with great shovelfuls of earth and fill the hole that he had had such a hard time digging two hours earlier and on which no one had bothered to compliment him.

No one had warned Bruno when he entered the big room. And who would have? How could he have imagined his mistress, the beautiful rich Luce Ader in her raw silk costume drying the dishes with a frightful cloth, and worse still, being ogled by a farmboy sprawled on his sordid alcove bed? Bruno was at first speechless, before managing to say:

"Luce, whatever's going on? Am I seeing straight, or are you doing the washing-up? Is this some new whim for Paris society to copy? You're, quite simply, grotesque, my darling."

Luce turned and gave him one of her lost, guilty looks which, as usual, exasperated Bruno to screaming pitch. But now that she'd put the cloth down on the table and was opening her mouth, an appalling sort of braying, the screams of a man or beast in agony shattered the room, causing him to retreat two paces.

"What on earth was that?" he stuttered.

His legs were trembling and he feared the yokel had noticed, but in fact he had turned his back to the room and appeared to be sleeping.

"It's the grandfather over there," the idiotic Luce finally said.

"Over there? Is he dangerous?"

The figure huddled like an old abandoned duster in the armchair had nothing disturbing about him, and Bruno felt reassured by this, but Luce wanted to make things clearer.

"He no longer has the teeth he needs to say his Ds

and his Ns, poor man. As he's very polite, he wants to say 'Good morning'. He tries and he says 'Ghee-maw." She spelt out G-H-E-E-M-A-W.

Feigning compassion, Bruno looked at her as though she were mad. But she continued quite unselfconsciously:

"You must answer him, Bruno. After all his efforts, it's the least you can do. The poor man must be very sensitive."

To make matters worse, the defective old man let out another frightful bray.

Luce was losing her patience.

"Go on, Bruno. He'll end up complaining to our hosts. What will we look like?"

"Good morning, monsieur," Bruno said in a normal voice, then, seeing Luce's expression, he practically bellowed "GOOD MORNING MONSIEUR" before turning to her:

"It's pathetic, can't you see. It's pathetic and revolting. Pack your cases, we're going. Where's Loïc? Still at the grave? What about Diane, is she digging too?"

He was trying to be funny, but only just managing. Seeing Luce at the sink had dumbfounded him. What was going on? How had these women been drawn into this lamentable farce? Had they been threatened? He went up to her:

"Luce," he said. "Is everything all right? How d'you come to be doing this? Has someone frightened you?"

"Frightened me? Who? D'you think Madame Henri has, who's been so kind? Or Maurice with his bad foot?" She blushed. "Or that poor old man who's lost all his teeth – and his marbles as well? You're joking, Bruno."

Luce took up the cloth again, shrugged her shoulders and looked sensible. Bruno began to laugh, but a low, wounding laugh, which he knew always upset her.

"So, my darling, was it your appendix they removed in Paris or your sense of the ridiculous? Your new personality will be a sensation in the States. Your husband won't recognize what a pearl of a house-wife, what a committed democrat he's got coming to him from Paris: a wife who weeps over chauffeurs, who nurses farmboys . . . who washes up. Perhaps you'd like to join the Communist Party as well, darling."

"You've got a husband! Now I'd never have believed that!" Apparently Maurice Henri was not asleep and his voice showed astonishment, if not vague disap-pointment.

Bruno was furious.

"Yes! Yes, my good fellow. Luce has a husband in Lisbon, and a lover – me . . . and several gentleman admirers in Paris. This is no innocent virgin you're sheltering, my good fellow. Sorry, I mean *Monsieur* Henri."

Even poor, peace-loving Luce could not fail to catch the venom inherent in "Monsieur".

"If I weren't smashed up the way I am, if I had my two legs, I'd break the bastard's jaw," Maurice muttered to some mysterious friend, or, anyway, to the hens sauntering by his bed.

He had kept his voice calm, which had given Diane the wrong impression, now that she entered the room in her wine-coloured flannel beach pyjamas and a bolero of pale pink cotton which emphasized her agitated bony form. She'd thought what Maurice was saying was part of an anecdote.

"Who was going to break whose jaw?" she asked.

"*I* was going to break that little cunt's jaw over there," Maurice repeated in the same slow voice, indicating Bruno with his chin.

Luce was uttering piercing little shrieks and waving her arms, and looked for all the world as though she were cackling and flapping wings. But the mimicry was undoubtedly unconscious.

Diane shrugged her shoulders, unperturbed. "I imagine you're joking."

At that point, Justice and Labour personified in the single form of Arlette-Memling arrived. She glanced at Bruno who was pouring himself some coffee and cutting a slice of bread.

"So you're on your feet at last?" she said. "Your friend Loïc's waiting for you in the yard to start the harvesting."

"I'm very sorry to disappoint you, dear Madame, but your harvesting will have to wait. I'm going into town to look for a car to relieve you of our company, and to find somewhere with more human life . . . If you don't mind?" he added with ironic deference.

Very slowly Arlette-Memling bent down and, from under his nose, withdrew the bowl and bread, which he was just about to consume with obvious hunger.

"Here, what we eat we earn," she said evenly, and walked off, leaving them aghast.

Bruno blenched, stood up, and kicked his chair over. The sun had reached the threshold. He stood there for a moment, trembling with heat and rage. But then, involuntarily, he retreated, terrified, his mind unable to conceive that the enormous war machine which was cutting across the yard in his direction, covered in dust and with all its blades clacking, was being driven by Loïc Lhermitte, until recently a diplomat at the Quai d'Orsay.

Loïc was returning from an hour's practice across the fields, after a lesson by Maurice. He had rarely been so amused; no racing car had ever excited him so much as this machine which cut, threshed the wheat and trussed the straw behind him.

Having performed an acrobatic descent, and reached firm ground again, he felt delighted with himself. The idiot's smiling, he's so pleased with himself, Bruno thought. Proud of himself and the wheat he's to cut, no doubt. For a moment Bruno was filled with despair. If he'd given up trying to make the two mad women see reason, he had at least hoped to find some mutual male support and simple good sense in Loïc.

"If you could just leave your roadster for a moment, dear fellow, I'd like to have a word."

"We'll talk later. Are you coming with me as far as the field?" Loïc asked, now that he had climbed back on to his chariot and was leaning down to him.

"Has Maurice explained what you have to do? I've hooked your clobber on behind. All you have to do is follow. Ah, dear Bruno, everything's been seen to," he said and started up the engine.

But Bruno stayed where he was, and made so violent a gesture of refusal, with such a contorted face, that Loïc stopped his machine again and cupped his ear.

"What's the matter?"

71

It would of course have been too simple for Bruno to do what was asked of him, just for once. He was too much of a snob to help these marvellous people with a bit of loading, people who were giving them shelter, feeding them and would continue doing so for several more days. Having been up to the top of the coomb and seen the sea of wheat, with only a thin line of bushes dividing it here and there, Loïc knew that any kind of departure was more than difficult. Even so, leaving here would be a far simpler matter than arriving somewhere else.

"Your new friend . . . our dear hostess, has just refused me a piece of bread," Bruno said, his teeth gritted in rage, ". . . so, I'm buggering off."

"What . . . she refused you bread?"

Loïc was visibly more astonished by what was refused than by the refusal itself.

"Why ever would she do that?"

"I don't know, but I've had enough. I'm going to take the pickup from down there and find a post office. A telephone must exist somewhere in France in 1940."

"The pickup's a write-off. I already asked Maurice this morning."

"Well, perhaps there's a bicycle then? Or I'll take one of the horses, or walk if necessary. You do understand, don't you, Loïc?"

Loïc sighed, resigned himself, and regretfully slid down from his command post. He patted Bruno on the shoulder.

"You're right. We must talk, old chap." He pushed him into the shade of the barn, lit a cigarette with cupped hands, in a virile gesture which exasperated

Bruno even more, like an additional betrayal. After all, since Loïc was past fifty, it should have been him who was the old moper, not Bruno, who was not even thirty. And yet it was actually Loïc who was being the adventurous one, the live-wire, the responsible person.

"Boo, boo, boo, boo . . . where are you then?" Diane's voice, then Diane herself joined them in her refined beachwear. All three stood in a semi-circle to plot their position. It had been a long time, Diane thought – since Luce was not there – that they could meet as serious people. They might even have qualified as normal company had Loïc not been there . . . or as well brought-up if Bruno had been absent. There was no end to the new qualities Diane was discovering in herself, thanks to everyone else's shortcomings.

"And you managed to pilot that enormous machine?" she asked Loïc with new respect.

"It's a most wonderful toy. You should try it, Diane."

But Bruno was in no mood to talk about toys.

"You saw, Diane, the way I was treated by that harpie and her cretinous son! I'm going to find a post office and telephone Ader, even if I have to walk. I hope you understand my position."

"But of course we do, dear Bruno. Of course. It's just . . . well, I did wonder, is it wise to set out with no map?"

Loïc and Diane seemed to have become normal and Bruno was glad at the change.

"I must find a way of getting to Orléans or Tours, or at least to a telegraph office. The pickup doesn't work."

Diane sighed: "Alas no, my poor friend. The Cro-Magnons are on foot these days. That said, all you have to do is walk in a south-westerly direction, that's all."

Arms folded over her frail charms, Diane seemed the very image of reason.

"South-westerly? God knows where that is," Loïc remarked.

"Over there."

Diane instantly shot out her arm towards a precise point in the impassive sky. The two men looked at her. She let her arm fall and said pityingly.

"I have . . . and God knows why, but they're two instinctive faculties I have. I know A. where the cardinal points of the compass are, and B. how to grow flowers. Green fingers and a sense of direction. I get it from my father who even crossed part of the Amazon when he was fifty – unknown territory till then."

"That at least proves the green fingers," Loïc said smiling, but Bruno looked at him suspiciously.

In the absence of any other information he had made his decision:

"I'm off, before that shrew chases me with a pitch-fork. My poor Diane," he said spiritedly, "when I think that Luce has even done the washing-up."

"Oh dear," Loïc and Diane shook their heads, eyes lowered.

"At least take a hat," Diane cried.

But he was already at the top of the coomb, and he was too alarmed by the countryside to hang around for something so trivial. He disappeared rapidly. And Diane exchanged sadistic smiles with Loïc.

"That'll calm him down," she said, and then, "when

all's said and done, if he finds somewhere to send a telegram from, so much the better."

"Would you like a little ride on my machine?"

Loïc was obsessed. Unable to resist, Diane the socialite climbed up on to the combine-harvester and did a very fast tour of the yard, screaming with fear and delight like a little girl. Then she let Loïc set off alone on his mission, to the fields of ripening corn awaiting him, and already trembling in apprehension.

They had only done a small trip of course, but, nevertheless, when Diane came back inside, she was reminded by Arlette-Memling that petrol did not come free.

As a consqunce or not of this mad frittering, the whole midday meal consisted of a small piece of fat bacon, some potatoes and some of the previous day's soup. Poor Loïc, already sunburnt and dripping with sweat, suffered more from it than the others. So much so that, profiting from the fact that Diane was giving the mistress of the house a lesson in antiques, and telling her the approximate age of her sideboard, he allowed himself to remove her portion of fat bacon and swallow it. Returning to her plate a moment later she used her knife, which until then she had been brandishing at the sideboard, to search for the delicious smoked ham she had left intact a moment before. In vain. She then dived under the table, ready to fight the hens for it, but it so happened they weren't there. She stood up again:

"Where's my ham?" she whispered severely.

"My God. Did you want it? I thought you'd left it. I'm really sorry," said the ambassadorial attaché, Chevalier

75

of the Legion of Honour, a man who subscribed to the Opera and was received everywhere as the best friend of the Sévignés among others.

"It's the first time anyone's done that to me," Diane declared, "and I find your attitude unworthy of a man of Society, and even of a man, full stop."

"It's also the first time I've done any harvesting," poor Loïc feebly defended himself.

Diane was devastated, her eyes bulged, but her acrimony and bitterness melted when she saw Loïc set off yet again towards his combine-harvester, stumbling with tiredness, visibly less enamoured of his machine and rather more attracted to his bed, in which direction he cast a long regretful look.

Meanwhile, it had been more than three hours since Bruno had set out to walk across country.

Chapter 5

Like many people in his *milieu*, Bruno needed an audience to make him feel he was someone, an audience which until then he'd always found everywhere. These witnesses to his existence were both part of the scenery, and an absolute necessity. And, subconsciously, he could not *not* imagine peasants huddling behind the scraggy bushes in this very flat landscape, watching him pass with admiration. This was why he set off at such a brisk pace: the picture of a smart gentleman in the country, looking sporty in his open-necked shirt, his head thrown back. Unfortunately, his head soon began to droop forwards as he made his way along a path full of uneven ruts and bumps, stones and weeds, which obliged him to leap, as if he were on the rocks at Fontainebleau. He felt the small stones through the soles of his Italian mocassins which, though perfect for the sloping plankwalks at Deauville, or the steps at Longchamps, now seemed too pliant, and even painful on these small paths.

Nevertheless, he walked without suffering too much for almost an hour, during which he must have covered three kilometres as the crow flies and many more besides, for three times he went to check whether small woods on either side might conceal a farmhouse, a telephone, or some means of transport. But in vain. At the end of an hour, the sight of a signpost in the distance spurred him on, but it was only to find two boards labelled "Mas Vignal" (Vignal Farm) and "La Tranchée" (The Trench). Bruno opted for La Tranchée, but after two hundred metres and thoughts too varied and too boring to record, decided Mas Vignal might be better. At one o'clock, he took off his mocassins. But walking in his socks was even more painful. He donned his shoes again. What sort of godforsaken place had he got into? He tried to remember what he knew of geography, but could find nothing in his memory of schooldays but some lines of a forgotten poem.

"Noon, King of summers, stretched o'er the plain,
Falls in sheets of silver from the high blue sky,
All is silent . . ."

Was it actually "stretched o'er the plain" or "lying o'er the plain"? He wasn't sure and it irritated him. His uncertainty gave his recitation an obsessive quality it had never had in class. It was hot, atrociously hot. He was sweating, but could not be bothered to wipe his forehead any more. The only minimally enjoyable moment was at two o'clock when he remembered the forgotten word: "spread".

"Noon, King of summers, spread o'er the plain."

That was it, he was sure. "Spread." He was also sure he was lost now. He couldn't go on. He began to see red lines under his eyelids, his pulse beat in his forehead like doors slamming. The group of trees he reached now, without any hope of finding whatever it was he was looking for – he was right about that anyway – the group of trees gave him a chance to lie in the shade; at first he lay on his back like a normal human being, then he turned on his stomach, crumpling his clothes, his head on his arms, on the verge of despair, exhaustion, sunstroke. There were no planes, no soldiers either in green or khaki, no battles . . . he had seen no one killed . . . Who was it who'd said France was still at war?

When he reached Mas Vignal, it was only to discover that the farm was obviously derelict. All that remained were the ruins of the farmhouse, a few scattered stones, a thicket of brambles, and three trees, under which he sat down once again. His feet were bleeding. He looked at them in a sort of stupor: his feet, beautifully pedicured only a week ago, were covered in blisters, callouses, burnt raw. He ached. He was hungry. He wanted to cry. Old tales of lost travellers, deserts and skeletons gnawed by jackals (or was it jackal?) passed through his mind. He could see the headlines in advance: "Young Handsome Bruno Delors found Dead, in Open Country in the Beauce". Ridiculous! Was Bruno Delors, such a favourite among the women, going to die in the Beauce? He had no wish for his death to be a cause of general mirth. Why should he be the only Frenchman to die in the Beauce? Not after escaping three aeroplanes and surviving an entire journey with the Fury Diane, that old maid Loïc and dopy Luce. And yet, thinking of them, tears of tenderness filled his eyes. He imagined them devastated by his disappearance, touring the farm looking for him, prisoners in this accursed countryside, prisoners in this accursed country of France. No, no one was going to recapture him here.

He began to cry quietly, holding back his louder sobs despite the silence and solitude that surrounded him implacably on every side. It was the first time he had truly understood the meaning of "implacable". In Paris, they used to talk about implacable people, implacable businessmen, implacable women. It was ridiculous. No one could be as implacable as the countryside, it was only the countryside that could be implacable.

Everything – his ideas, his head, the ground – was spinning. To cut a long story short, on this fine June day in 1940, Bruno Delors lay spreadeagled on good French soil, and wept for a long time about himself, for he wasn't to know that Marshal Pétain was in the act of signing an armistice with the German army just a hundred kilometres away, and so could not weep over that.

Bruno, then, was in serious conflict with the country-side, a victim of brutally severe sunstroke, when a simple-minded farmboy found him lying under the group of trees. It was nearly three in the afternoon, when Nochance came across him in his leafy bower, snoring, whistling and murmuring peculiar words in a high-pitched voice, his face scarlet, his limbs twitching. Nochance, who was on his way home, stopped.

Nochance was a village boy whose name was Jean like everyone else's. Born of an unknown father whom he still had, and a poor woman who had died after giving birth to him, thirty years later Jean owed his nickname to a drinking session which had taken place one evening when he was fifteen (but already looked twice if not three times as old), when his drunken friends had called him Nochance, a nickname born of Jean's immediate response to anything mentioned to him by anyone, whether it was hunting, marriage, drinking, women or politics. The nickname had stuck, and since his parents' had gone, there were only a few old women who, seeing him cross the fairground, could say: "Look, there goes Jean". But they never added their usual: "There's a little boy who'll go a long way", because everyone knew he was going nowhere. In fact they also called him "Meningou", an old dialect word which, when contracted, had come to mean meningitis. The few bouts he had had of this still showed in his shambling posture, even if his life had been spared.

Meningou began to admire the sleeping man's beautiful effects, and in his innocence tried to remove his watch, failed, and awakened Bruno, who propped himself up on his elbows, feverish and haggard. He saw an out-of-focus face, and even after blinking it remained so. For Meningou had all the signs of a somewhat accentuated mental illness, a kind of imprecision in his features and facial contours, as if he had been made in stipplework. His eyes and mouth never laughed together; it always seemed that the feeling expressed in his face was never the same as the one he was experiencing, and this made it hard for people to take him seriously and consequently to love him.

Meningou therefore lived alone in a ruined house behind a thicket. Some unformed and exaggerated sexual impulses had at one time led him to assault a village woman, a powerful creature who, even while

81

he was attempting to rape her, had strung him up in her doorway by his trouser belt before he could have his way, and, afterwards, through an understandable error, he'd assaulted a curate, a frail young man whom the parish priest was trying to harden to country life and whom Meningou's all too pressing attentions obliged to move to a more urban apostolate. Whether or not he was sated by these transgressions, for five years Meningou had remained quiescent: public opinion had it that he satisfied himself with a few domestic animals, even though not once had a single animal among those great flocks been seen to tremble, call out or trot in his direction at the sight of him. It was therefore thought that Meningou not only interfered with but also chastized the objects of his desire, which inevitably made the poor beasts cynical and undemonstrative.

To cut a long story short, Nochance fell instantly in love with this fine young man lying in the grass, with his beautiful clothes and crimson face. Overwhelmed, he stretched out his hand to Bruno, touched his hair and pulled it playfully, a light trail of saliva spilling on to his lower lip. On other occasions and in other places Bruno would have screamed in horror, tried to punch this pervert and run for dear life. But he was delirious. And his delirium was peopled with deserts, sand, eternal dunes, unfindable oases and benevolent nomads. Admittedly, the man standing before him did not present the noble face of the Kabyle tribe or Blue Men, but he seemed happy and proud to have saved him from an atrocious and, without him, inescapable death. Bruno stood up, swayed, and had to lean on his companion. His temperature was 41 degrees, he could see tarbooshes and dromedaries everywhere, and smilingly accepted the mad kisses with which Meningou was devouring his face, as ancestral Musulman practices. Bruno, in turn, planted a few, more modest, kisses on the astonishingly fleshy, pink cheeks of his Bedouin, this thick-skulled son of the desert – and here one can say that even the most blasé of Parisians would have been astounded by the scene. Quickly tiring of these old customs, nevertheless, Bruno sat down Turkish fashion on the stony ground, with legs crossed and feet tucked under his thighs. This new mode of sitting which Nochance had never seen practised in the Beauce – and for good reason – increased his respect and admiration. He tried to sit likewise, tripped and fell, and after several graceless and unsuccessful attempts, was resigned to sitting in his usual manner at the feet of his new lover.

Bruno, who in his fever was dying of thirst, waited a few moments for the mint tea, that inevitably mild, sugary drink of North Africa – he knew it well – and seeing nothing come, questioned his saviour.

"I thirsty," he said. "I hungry, I ill. You take me to next fort."

This polished, succinct language, though it may have astonished him, was perfectly attuned to Nochance's brain. He stood up, content.

"I lead you," he said firmly . . . "We eat cassoulet of Mother Vignol. You have money?" And he shook his pockets to make his request clear, so that when Bruno saw what he was doing he stood up and smiled.

"I have plenty gold in Paris . . . but I know you despise money."

This discourse did not strike much of a chord with Nochance.

"We need money for cassoulet," he said with visible anguish.

Bruno tried to be reassuring.

"I owe you my life. I offer you friendship, faith, confidence. I cut off my hand for you. But I not give you filthy banknotes. I know you despise banknotes."

"But yes, yes, I accept banknotes from you," Nono reassured him with uncommon vigour.

"I give you later. Everything – everything. What you want now?"

"Your watch."

In spite of his stupidity and ignorance, the boy had noticed that Bruno's clothes were unwearable and torn, and he only had one brilliant thing on him: his watch. Bruno vaguely recollected that this was a platinum watch and it had cost night after night with an ancient English baroness. He tried feebly to defend it.

"My watch worth twenty camels," he said emphatically. "Twenty camels and kilos and kilos of dates."

"Meno like dates," Nono said, holding out his hand.

And Bruno, with aching heart, took off his watch. But it was at this moment that his Parisian friends arrived in the cart, whose approach had been hidden by the line of trees: Luce and Loïc, accompanied by Arlette Henri, had finally begun to wonder about Bruno's disappearance. Arlette had harnessed the horses and had had no difficulty following Bruno's tracks in the dust.

"Give him back his watch," she shouted at Nochance. "Did you steal it? If you don't want to go to prison, you can come home with us and help with the harvesting.

84

Come to the farm, I'll give you something to eat after the wheat's been cut tomorrow," Madame Memling cried purposefully, having noted Nochance's strong sun-tanned arms. "Come and finish the harvesting Nochance. I'll pay you."

Normally he would have replied "No chance!" to propositions such as harvesting and field work. But now, as his lover, his discovery, was here, he had to follow him.

"Have we arrived at the fort or the frontier? What tribe is my saviour speaking to?" asked Bruno to a shadow with a burnous wrapped round its legs, failing to recognize the affectionate voices and faces, however dear, which surrounded him. They thought you lost, these faces said, they were afraid. It was up to him to relieve the tension and reassure them.

"I prefer couscous to cassoulet," he said. "I lover of desert. I follow your caravan," he said to one named "Al Lett", a severe-faced native dressed in a black kaftan.

A little later he was lying in the cart returning to the Henris' farm, with Luce's guilty, tear-stained hand in his. Taking advantage of his lethargic state, Loïc would swipe him across the cheek every so often, under the pretext of reviving him. Swipes which made Bruno regret the more enveloping and tender customs of his friend the Tuareg, who had become invisible, but who in fact was placidly cleaning his teeth with a stem of grass, and dangling his legs over the side of the cart.

As for Arlette Henri, who was managing the horses, she glanced back at her little group dead with fatigue, and congratulated herself on her arrangements, particularly on having managed to persuade Nochance, the most pigheaded man in the village, to work in her fields. When he was willing (and it was many years since anyone had succeeded in persuading him), he did the work of ten. Maurice would be happy, she said to herself. And Loïc, whose back was to her, thought he heard her humming an old, half-forgotten song called "Fascination" . . . "I met you . . . simply . . ."

But he was so tired that it did not even make him smile, and afterwards he thought he had dreamed it. In any case, it did not last long, for, turning towards the back of the cart and jerking her chin at Bruno, she said to Loïc: "Don't worry. Tomorrow he'll be on his feet."

What she meant was: on his feet with a fork.

Chapter 6

Diane had excused herself from the rescue mission, on the pretext of waiting for Bruno at the house, should he return on his own. The real reason was she had not finished the chore Arlette had set her, and could not bring herself to admit it. This was probably due to childish pride, she thought as she pottered about by herself. Her job was simple but unpleasant: she had to sort a crate of apples: put the bitter ones on one side and the sound ones on the other. Judging them by eye, and, if that failed, by biting.

"I'll make some tarts tomorrow for the harvesters' pudding," Arlette said to her. "We'll have to have three big ones. Mine are the best, so the men say. Oh, you've come to good home cooking here," she announced to a startled Diane.

Now that Diane was doing her sorting-out away from public gaze, and had put on her spectacles, she scrutinized each apple intently, but to no avail: there was no way she could tell its quality. And so, she frequently had to bite them. She'd applied herself to this with great zeal at first, but gradually she changed to using only the very tips of her teeth, for, as the acid from the apples violently attacked her gums, her teeth threatened to ache; one or two were even coming loose. Her speed of selection, so bedevilled till now, had consequently tailed off. And as Arlette-Memling passed behind her, with her arms full of various implements, she'd cuttingly remarked:

"Tell me, you poor soul, are you going to spend all night at it? I usually puts my tarts in the oven in the evening. You'd better not fall asleep on the job."

"I simply can't tell one apple from another."

"I already told you, you got to bite them."

"But I can't bite every apple in three whole kilos. Three of my teeth have come loose already," Diane whimpered in a voice that was more desperate than rebellious, for gone was her "childish pride": the farmer's wife well and truly terrified her.

"Bad workmen always blames their tools. Go on, you'll manage it. Parisians is smart," the farmer's wife said and concluded with a smile, albeit a fleeting one, for she immediately added:

"Pay attention though. It only needs one bad apple for the whole tart to taste rotten."

Leaving Diane in a state of terror, Madame Memling moved off to do her daily chores and prepare her feast for the morrow, while in the big room Luce had been landed with washing up the crockery stored in the sideboard since the last harvest in 1939, and now covered in dust and rat droppings. Just think, Diane told herself, before doing the dishes, Luce had to collect the eggs, and mix the feed for the ducks. Poor Luce. Stupidly, she had rushed through everything, done too much, tried to surpass herself and, every time her work was finished, she'd been given more chores to do. She,

Diane, at least, had stayed glued to her apples and at the end of the day would come out without too many aches and pains (even if she had acquired several mouth ulcers and a slight nausea with all that excessive secretion of gastric juices). And all for a lunch the purpose of which had absolutely no interest to her. And so despite the possible humiliation, here she was waiting to welcome Bruno's triumphal return. But could one count on a dandy like him in these dramatic circumstances? It was easy to see that there was a war on. She was well aware of that now. It had needed a nationwide, or worldwide, catastrophe to justify the social collapse of which she and Luce had been victims for the last two days, and to explain the respectful attention she gave to the diktats of a peasant woman.

A little later, the noise of the cart in the yard tore Diane from her reveries and her chore, like an emigrée hearing the sinister tumbrils reentering the Temple. Mortified and defiant, she swiftly mixed the bitter apples in with the good, had time to tear off her black smock apron which went round her twice, and emerged from the cellar. Outside, Loïc and Luce were supporting Bruno as they brought him into the house, where they sat him on the only remotely comfortable chair in the big room. Bruno was swaying backwards and forwards. Nothwithstanding the extreme flatness of the countryside, the poor unfortunate must have had a bad fall. Loïc enlightened her:

"It's just the blasted sunstroke, I swear, Diane. He's not at any risk."

"You always gets sunstroke here in the summer,

because there's not enough trees," Maurice Henri said reassuringly; even so, he looked pretty smug now that he could see the piteous state his rival had returned in.

He was superb with his suntan, and though his body had been left white where his vest had been, the effect was in fact more disturbing than ugly.

"What happened to him, then? Where did you find him?" Diane's voice sounded like a cross between a judge's and a reporter's.

Loïc turned round: "We found him under a tree, where this young man had carried him."

He pointed to the individual accompanying them, who seemed ageless, brainless and soulless, and was muttering:

"'Day Madame," in a high-pitched squeak, that was unnerving coming from a youth of his size and strength.

"Good day, monsieur."

Her clarion voice proclaimed both her attachment to social niceties and the handicaps life inflicted on them from time to time. "I thank you then, monsieur, on behalf of all my friends, for having brought him back to us . . . My God," she cried, catching sight of Bruno's face. "What a state he's in. Did you have to drag him out of a beehive or something?"

Bruno's dark, swollen face was frightening and disturbing. His sudden ugliness not only transformed but depersonalized him, dehumanized him almost. He relied so heavily in life on his physique and his good looks that he seemed suddenly to have become a nowhere man, with no past, and worst of all, no future

90

. . . What would become of poor Bruno Delors if he stayed like this? You would only have to look in the clinics, the hostels, the hospices – somewhere ghastly in any case – for an answer.

"Bee hive, bee hive!" the newcomer repeated. "Beehive. No chance. Nochance no go near one."

"There you are," Maurice declared to his mattress, as if filled with joy by these words. "It's all he knows how to say: 'No chance. No chance.' That's why he nicknamed Nochance."

Diane was used to nicknames (God knows they were prolific enough in her circle), but this one disconcerted her.

"It's not very charitable," she said severely.

"The women call him Meningou as well, you could call him that instead," Maurice continued. "He had something in his brain when he was little, an illness called meningitis, a . . . well, anyway, they called him Meningou."

"Ghee-maw, ghee-maw," the old man brayed at that precise moment; apparently his hearing was improving daily, and he had noticed a new voice in the chorus of his entourage, that had been so agreeably augmented of late.

"G'day, Monsieur Henri, G'day Monsieur Henri," the aforementioned Nochance winked at Bruno as if to share the subject of his hilarity with his good friend, but to no avail, for Bruno's head had fallen onto his chest.

What a state the elegant clothes he'd been wearing that morning were in now, thought Diane. And she caught Loïc glancing at him too, making a woeful inventory of the damage.

"We must put him to bed," said Arlette-Memling, who had silently entered and was now lifting Bruno's chin and staring him out, her eyes as cold as a Sioux's. "He's going to be feverish and coughing up all over the place, and then tomorrow he'll be on his feet again, as good as new."

She absentmindedly patted the invalid's cheek, with all the sensitivity she'd pat a cow's. It was then that Nochance bent over Bruno and planted a big kiss on his haggard eyes, before casting a bestial look of collusion at the Parisians, that made them recoil in horror.

"What on earth's he up to?" Diane cried.

For once Diane was less shocked by the suitor's social class than by his intentions.

'Will you leave him alone," she called out again, while Loïc grabbed him by the collar to prevent him repeating his demonstration of affection.

"Nochance. Let him be," Maurice Henri cried, adding his strong male voice to the attempt to stop him, but a voice choking with laughter, which forced him to double up on his mattress, his eyes glittering with tears.

"It's true, you've no right," Luce shouted with unexpected courage.

Nochance retreated and, lowering his head, murmured,

"He really wanted to, just now . . ." then spluttered some other lie, which only served to alienate everyone.

The burning question now was: had Nochance taken advantage of their young friend's weak state to . . . to . . . abuse him? What a sweet revenge for all those women Bruno had despoiled, Diane thought – even though she was glutting her lust for revenge at a time when he was hardly being demanding, and that did him a disservice. Women who paid for their pleasure never enjoyed paying a small price: they would accuse their lover of smallmindedness or stupidity, never of being considerate – consideration disappeared for them the moment the first bit of cash changed hands.

Subtle and profound reflexions on her circle, such as these, filled Diane's mind, while Nochance and Loïc carried Bruno to his bed, followed by Luce, looking pale and penitent in advance. Meanwhile Maurice Henri buoyantly lit a cigarette and threw himself down on his alcove bed.

Loïc looked perplexedly at Nochance, torn between horror and the giggles, at the idea of such a virile, arrogant and snobbish man as Bruno teaming up with this idiot fellow. At first sight it was crazy, but when it came to relationships (as had often been said), anything was possible. If it was sunstroke that had sparked off this lightning attraction, one could only hope for the best in a situation involving someone like Bruno Delors, who was for ever vaunting his heterosexuality, but was now smiling encouragement at a village idiot.

Loïc found the prospect of this idyll irresistible: not that he loathed Bruno, nor that he thought the whole episode disreputable, but he was aware of the conflict with Bruno's deeply felt and firmly rooted convictions and those of many others. His sexual preferences had given him an unshakable superiority. Loïc could become a minister, save ten children from a fire and die in the process, discover a cure for cancer or paint a Mona Lisa, but there would always come a point in the conversation when Bruno could turn the laughter to his advantage, and at Loïc's expense. It would be less likely, of course, if Loïc were to make a fortune.

Alone with the Henris, Diane and Luce had a moment of extreme discouragement and irresolution: the vagaries of their fate and their efforts at saving their dignity had drained them almost completely. And their relationship which had been founded securely on a certain way of life suddenly wavered and became amorphous, lacking feeling or grace. And even, if, in their conversations or their interior monologues, they retained a certain pride, at night in bed, Diane, like Loïc and Bruno before, would wonder: "What am I doing here?" "What's going to become of us?" "Who among these people likes me?" etc., etc., etc. In short, they were at last face to face with themselves; they had no sleeping pills to take, nor could they have even the shortest of telephone conversations with another equally insomniac friend.

And so Luce was the only one to remain calm, apart from her attraction to Maurice, and the fact that her "mother-in-law", if that was the right description for this wild woman, her mother-in-law frightened the life out of her. She blushed with gratitude when Arlette said gruffly:

"You've worked real hard. 'Tis all scrubbed in here, it glows. And the dishes is really clean. 'Tis just that there'll be about twenty of us tomorrow . . . Have you finished the apples?" she asked in a less amiable tone as she turned to Diane.

"I've finished your apples, or almost," Diane said courageously. "My mouth's all sore inside, and I've

94

even cut my finger," she announced, proudly displaying a small gash on her thumb.

Loïc reappeared from the bedroom corridor, looking amused again. He was being quite useful as well as entertaining and jolly during their hellish stay, Diane thought. The tan he'd acquired on top of the combine-harvester really suited him, he'd lost that soft, indecisive look which in Paris had made him sometimes seem unattractive.

He sat down beside her, picked up a glass from the table and having glanced at Madame Cro-Magnon for approval, filled it at the tap and drank.

Once Arlette had decamped, Luce innocently went to sit beside Maurice. Soon nothing could be seen of her but her narrow back; her head and shoulders were deep in the alcove, where she was undoubtedly closely tending the wounded. Loïc and Diane were left in peace.

"So, what's been happening?" Diane whispered. "D'you think Bruno . . .?"

"All I can say is, they have a very affectionate form of meningitis around here."

"Ghee-maw, ghee-maw?"

"And were they in one another's arms when you found them? What an incredible story. Is Bruno a faggot. then?"

Was "faggot" the right term? Perhaps it was "fish queen" she was thinking of. But no, what did "fish queen" mean exactly, as the expression floated up through her memory and finally popped out through the surface like an old branch?

"They weren't embracing at all, Diane. I never said

that . . . Bruno was sitting Turkish fashion, with his legs crossed under him, and a blank expression on his face, and Noway . . ."

"Nochance!" Diane corrected him severely.

"As you wish. Nochance was sitting on his buttocks in the French manner, his eyes blazing. But there was nothing equivocal in that until that kiss we all saw here. And another in the bedroom, I'm afraid. Bruno hasn't recognized me, but he's smiled at his suitor."

"You see. It's true, it's true."

Diane was exultant.

"Had Bruno gone far? How far away was he when you found him?"

"Oh, about eight kilometres."

"He'd taken four hours to go eight kilometres? No, he must have been dawdling – and Nochance had been flirting with him."

"Flirting?" (Loïc laughed.) "Flirting. There's nothing flirtatious about Nochance."

"Ghee-maw, ghee maw."

"Belt up," Loïc shouted irritatedly.

He turned to Diane:

"What a bore than man is."

"No one could say you lack spunk," Diane said, bedazzled.

"What if Arlette hears you?"

"Ghee-maw, ghee-maw."

"Leave him, poor old thing. He's bored in his chair."

Luce had emerged from the alcove with a red face and hair all awry, and Loïc held up an admonishing finger, then turned to Diane.

"Well, what about you, what've you been doing all day, my dear. You must have been bored."

"Bored? I would've loved to have been bored. No, Arlette made me sort and re-sort the apples all afternoon. I didn't dare refuse, we make work for her and after all she has no domestic help at all, it seems to me," she murmured, ashamed of her cowardice. Loïc went on:

"Well, I did quite well with my infernal machine, even though it did cut down two or three trees in the process. But the best of it was that it well and truly reaped, threshed and baled two chickens. They came out the other end wildly protesting and shaved smooth, with no feathers left to ruffle."

"Where are they? Find them, do, Loïc," Diane begged. "I'm supposed to pluck two for this famous lunch tomorrow, with the Henris and their neighbours the Faberts. Arlette wants to make me kill two of them myself."

"How on earth will you do that?"

"I've asked Maurice for his hunting gun. I hope there's enough shot left in it for me to kill them tomorrow morning."

"Ghee-maw, ghee-maw."

"Will you dry up, you silly old chatterbox," Diane shouted sharply, but stopped dead when Arlette emerged from the corridor: there was every chance she might have heard.

So what! Diane thought. She wouldn't eat any more, she'd stay in her bed and die of hunger, like an animal, but a free animal at least.

However, Arlette wasn't interested in listening, no

more was she interested in seeing Luce's face, whose colour, expression and hair said all there was to be said. Loïc continued:

"One of us should go and keep watch on our friend Nochance: he's all alone with Bruno."

"I'll go," Diane offered, and she trotted off, delighted with her role of duenna.

She still could not truly believe what was going on. Not that Bruno's morals appeared unshakable to her, but there was something which wasn't right. God knows, though, how many scandals she had known – her world was never lacking in them. She'd seen a young bridegroom run off on his wedding day with his bride's brother, and all of them take cover at the thermal baths at Saint-Honoré; she'd seen the wife of a Prime Minister leave him on the quayside and go off with his yacht and the bellboy from the hotel; she'd seen a very rich Italian prince disinherit all his family for a florist. But the same rules were respected. A rich man always ran off with a rich woman, or a rich partner with a poor one, never two poor people together. That couldn't ever lead to anything. Who'd still invite a poor man, who wasn't on his own any more and wouldn't be any use as an escort, or a poor woman who wasn't on her own either who'd be useless as a confidante in town, or as a companion on tedious journeys? In short, neither one nor the other of these parasitic adventurers would be received, and they would disappear into the shadows from whence they had come. But was there any reason why one would ever forsake an old acquaintance, one's equal at the Stock Exchange, for the sake of two nonentities who'd never appreciated the opportunity they'd been given.

In short, a gigolo like Bruno would surely never go off with a shepherd boy like Nochance, unless he was suicidal, ridiculous and indecent.

If this defective young man had been heir to a steelworks, then of course everything would have been different: that would have given some rationale to the thing, including abandoning Luce. But this whole episode, frankly, was too sordid, too doomed to failure and mediocrity, no one was amused by it any more.

And thus it was with the intention of giving him a lecture in morals that Diane entered Bruno's bedroom – he was still as flushed and feverish as ever, she saw, and still being watched over by his suitor, perched at the foot of the bed.

Diane nodded amiably and sat opposite him: they were like two firedogs fixed on either side of the bed, but the absurdity of the scene no longer mattered to Diane: she had rediscovered her role as a woman of Society and its inherent obligations. She had to get to the very bottom of this affair, she had to know everything, even if it had to be through Notachanceinhell. Time was on her side: there was no question of skinning or plucking anything whatsoever this evening.

"Our friend seems a lot better," she began smilingly.

Out of the Parisians, the older woman was also the most frightening in Nochance's view, and had scared him ever since the cart had arrived at the farm. The pretty young woman seemed quite shy and the big thin man was too quiet. But this female with her red hair was the sort who made trouble. What was it she was asking now, for example? Demanding to know with that shrill voice of hers? He understood nothing of what she was saying to him, with all those words . . . Nochance decided to resort to simplified language which, as he'd learnt that very morning from his friend, could be used equally well for Parisians as for Red Indians.

"Me no understand," he said.

Diane snorted. Right then. This poor fellow's talking pidgin now. Orléans however was closer than Timbuctoo . . . "Oh France, mother of the Arts, men and trees," she recited from memory. Oh, if only those fine poets, like Péguy or that other man . . . Claudel, with their overwhelming obsession for ploughed fields and bell towers, could do a tour of the Beauce. Then they would realize how fortunate they'd been. It would give her great pleasure to take them round. They would then appreciate how different these peasants were from their stereotypes. That said, she was exaggerating: Nochance was defective through an accident. He had had meningitis, everyone knew that. Everyone in the Beauce knew that, she thought. She was being dishonest. She adopted a prudent, honeyed, barely ironic tone, which she reserved for certain doubtful cases, and began:

"Me ask if Bruno feeling better?"

Nochance sighed. At least she was talking the same language as the other people now, well, what was it she'd called him? He pointed his finger at the pillow.

"He Bruno?"

"Yes, of course, he Bruno. Bruno Del . . . well, he Bruno."

It was useless making more complete introductions, it might even prove dangerous for later. Although Diane

100

could not imagine Nochance resorting to blackmail in Avenue Foch. No. No. It was simply horrible that he didn't know Bruno's name and they'd given themselves to each other without being introduced first. It was so bestial. Like a couple of animals. For it was definitely a lover's look the boy was giving Bruno. What a secretive little person he was! She wondered how long he'd harboured these leanings. Perhaps they only came to the surface in the country? Which would explain his revulsion for the farm. Unless he'd been assaulted and raped? But no, he'd smiled at this degenerate creature. It was imperative therefore that she finish her enquiry. Even if it progressed only through onomatopoeia.

"You met Bruno where?"

"Me found him Vignal Wood."

"He how?"

"He laid on ground on beautiful clothes."

"You think him nice?"

"Yes, him very nice. More nice than curate."

"Than who?"

"Him more nice than curate. You not know curate?"

"Not here, no. Now you, what to do?"

"Me wake him."

"To tell him what?"

"He want me take him to fort."

"Where?"

"To fort."

"What fort? Well? Did you say yes?"

"Yes, me say yes."

Etc, etc, etc.

The rest of the dialogue between the young degenerate of the lower Beauce and an overexcited Parisienne from the highest society yielded nothing of truly great interest, and revealed neither to one nor the other anything of the customs or the language of their respective tribes.

Loïc Lhermitte had never had to endure such physical tiredness before, which, for a nervous disposition like his, was proving a blessing. He had not felt so well for a long time. Once he'd reached the top of the track, he'd left the coomb and was lying on a pile of straw that his combine-harvester had shed on their return. He had taken from his bag a litre bottle of Arlette's chilled red wine, which tasted of grapes, and had lit himself a coarse, yellowish cigarette. He was now stretched out on his back, with bits of straw tickling his neck, a bitter taste of grape in his throat and his mouth burning with nicotine; he was experiencing a voluptuousness and pleasure in life that he couldn't ever recall feeling before. The silence of the fields, broken only by the increasingly lively chatter of birds scattered around him as the sun sank, trickled gently in his ears. The smell of wheat, which he'd cut himself, was doubly intoxicating both for its acrid smell and fumes and the fact that it was his responsibility; he was close to regretting a whole lifetime in the countryside he had not had. Which, he also discovered, in no way resembled those eternal weekends in Austria or Deauville.' Provence or the Sologne to which he had been invited for so many years. Was it being alone as he was now that he had missed before? Or the accessories which he'd been given then – croquet mallets, dinghies, rackets, guns – which failed to amuse him? Perhaps he was only inspired by the combine-harvester, this imposing, fearsomely noisy machine. But where could he have found one before and with whom? He had a hard time imagining asking Bill Careman or the dear dowageï Duchess d'Epinal to lend him their threshing machine and farm over a weekend. These pastoral moments were for ever leaving him astonishing, imperishable memories, like Luce feeding the ducks or Diane sorting apples, or even poor Bruno being brought back unconscious by the village idiot. Yes, they would have some good anecdotes to tell. But, to his own surprise, he felt less a sense of pleasure than of nostalgia. Rather than commenting on his past, he would have preferred to prolong the present. In fact he wanted to stay here more than go on to New York. Even if he found it difficult to admit, he had the impression that, physically and morally, some knot inside him had been untied, that he had recovered freedom of limbs and mind, and sloughed off his old personality among the parties and balls in Paris: that dry as dust, starchy Loïc Lhermitte who was so completely limited and predictable and who would have preferred to go with the others to New York, was a personality he no longer needed or wanted. The new Loïc on the other hand preferred to stay here, either on this or some other farm, or embark on *Two Children's "Tour de France"* again, a book he'd adored at school like all children of that age.

He was drawn from his bliss by a noise which was not rural, and wriggled on his stomach to the edge of the coomb and looked over. He was above the roofs of the farm, quite near the barn, and it was through its windows with their slanting beams that he saw two intertwined shadows, two fleshy silhouettes he quickly recognized as Luce and Maurice. The latter must have overcome his pain, as Luce her fear, and taking advantage of poor Bruno's inert state, they were at last able to give physical expression to the very real desire they felt for one another. Loïc could not and did not try to see much from his position, for the last of the sun's rays were glinting on the barn, only occasionally illuminating a golden red body which would then be extinguished as it rolled in the hay. But though he may not have seen much, he could, on the other hand, hear Luce's amorous voice: a firm, immodest voice, the voice of a woman who was yielding to pleasure with unexpected dynamism and decision. He'd imagined Luce cold and passive, in any case hardly the sensual type. It seemed he was wrong, hugely wrong.

In fact, he was not wrong and neither was Diane, even if this voice would have surprised her too. It had been a long time since Luce had cried out or reached a climax like this. She had one of those rare temperaments which preferred the other person not to interfere much when they were making love: she detested the man being attentive and taking precautions, and achieved her pleasure only when her partner ignored her. Her kind liked rough trade; any form of refinement was useless, real lovers made them feel ill at ease and constrained them, while unsophisticated ones gratified them. This is what her husband had discovered and was why he had married her, for with his own attraction to soubrettes, he had seen in her one of the few Society women he could pleasure without spending too much time on it. He tired of her after a while but he tired of all women anyway. Luce had then given herself to conscientious Parisian lovers, who were concerned about their mistress's pleasure and, because of this, prevented it.

Maurice had an old-fashioned attitude: girls tumbled in the hay for his pleasure. Some enjoyed themselves as a result, others less so, but he didn't even think about it. He offered his virility, his vigour, but no technique or self-control. He did what he had to do for his own pleasure – which was great – and so much the better if the women got some for themselves at the same time: he did not indulge in other roundabout methods.

That didn't always please. And so Luce's ecstatic, flagrant pleasure astonished him, filled him with wonder, in some sort of way; the prostitutes he'd bought barely feigned it and the girls he'd seduced were not, as far as sensuality went, as altruistic and unorthodox as Luce. When Luce saw this handsome boy working himself to the bone on her, getting excited and moving about inside her without even seeming to notice her, it blew her mind. It was such a miraculous change from Bruno who, in spite of his animality, never stopped observing her or listening to her (probably conscious of his career or his vocation, or more likely his vanity), and saying to her at absolutely the wrong moment, "Tell me what you want me to do", "Do you like it like that, eh?" etc., so many words reminding her of herself, that is, of someone other than him, and infuriating her. In short, Maurice's selfish, violent and, until then, solitary pleasure struck her like lightning, and she cried out under him as she had never cried out under anyone before.

105

It was, thank God, that time in the evening, when chickens and ducks joined in the wild birds' chorus of alarm as darkness fell, and their commotion was at its noisiest. The lovers' cries of passion were masked – it was mundane to say this – by the quack-quacks, cluck-clucks, pitter-patters and other forms of fowl-like expression prevailing in the yard. Pigs, donkeys and a few cows mingled their lower-pitched calls in this devout, discreet concert, this reaction of animal modesty, which, like Russian choirs, hid the crudeness or the horror of events from others less involved. Only Loïc, who was closest to the lovers, had all the leisure to listen to these voluptuous cries, and while he was not aroused by them, he at first felt astonished, then happy. For he was very fond of Luce; as was the way in his circle, where some of the more perceptive men liked and pitied certain beautiful, stupid women for whom they had no desire themselves.

The sun set, disappearing below the horizon, at the end of this very long flat plain, stretching so far that you could guess or imagine the earth's curve. It had to curve, had to turn at some point or other, very far away, to prevent it going on and on in the same way. If it did not, it would, in its undeviating trajectory, hit something like a cloud or the sun even. It looked as though it was getting rounder and, in fact, following Galilean principles. Taking its time, hour by hour, minute by minute, the sun had very gently begun its agony: first immersed to the waist, then the shoulders, it was as though some impatient hand were now pulling it violently into the depths. Its fall accelerated, diluted into pinks, its dome grew smaller and smaller and sank.

A red light still flashed occasionally from its bald pate, which had now turned almost black. Then its head seemed to emerge again triumphantly, or desperately, at any rate tragically, for one last time, to gaze upon the earth, before being suddenly immobilized, merged with the horizon, disappearing or whatever. The birds were silent; evening weighed heavy upon the earth; and to Loïc, lying on his side after the day's harvesting, the earth appeared entirely like one of Victor Hugo's poems. He had learnt this long poem at school years ago, he had even been able to recite it in its entirety to his bedazzled family, it was all a very long time ago. But now, at the beginning of a second world war and fifty years on, Loïc Lhermitte could only recall the first line:

"Boaz had lain down, overcome with exhaustion."

When he reentered the big room ten minutes later – for he wanted to spare the lovers from arriving last – he found all the little family at the table, a steaming tureen enthroned at its centre, and Madame Memling standing with ladle in hand, watched emotionally by Luce, Diane and Maurice. Everyone was dying of hunger, including himself. He took his seat, unhurriedly nevertheless, next to Diane, and was relieved to see the huge hunk of bread hidden behind his plate.

"Shall I serve the workers first, or the invalid?" Arlettc said, plunging the ladle in. She drew out a mass of vegetables, leeks, potatoes, carrots, plus an enormous piece of fat bacon which she carefully placed on Loïc's plate first, and he was astonished how satisfied he felt. With the same generosity she then served her son, Luce and Diane, then herself, each ladleful being a merit point for work, and each received it as such, pink with confusion and with eyes lowered, Loïc noticed (he was the only one of his group to have retained some independence). Since hunger and the great pleasure of eating had removed all his faculties of observation, it was only after finishing his plate that he noticed how different Luce and Maurice, seated next to one another, looked. Pleasure had all at once suffused them with a softness, a smoothness, a radiance, and they were constantly making efforts not to touch one another – efforts which Loïc found more revealing than all the familiar, intimate gestures of blatant lovers.

Maurice was joking, his eyes creased with laughter and very recent pleasure. Luce said nothing but smiled at what he was saying, not looking directly at him, but with a dignified, indulgent expression, the opposite of the clumsy, anxious woman he knew. It was so obvious, that Diane kept glancing at them suspiciously. But, naturally, without realizing the truth. She had most probably returned none the wiser from her visit to the invalid, and was now feeling exasperated. She leant over to Loïc, then changed her mind and addressed the mistress of the house direct:

"Are there any fortresses round here, Arlette?"

"Fortresses? What d'you call fortresses?" For once Maurice, who was never fazed, looked astonished. "What d'you mean? Like forts but bigger?"

"Yes, like that."

"Well no," Maurice said. "What would we be doing with fortresses? This is the Beauce, here."

"We're not exactly on the Maginot Line my dear," Loïc began, intrigued.

But she looked rattled and irritated by his intervention.

"Who's talking about the Maginot Line, Loïc? I'm just trying to find out, asking if there were any fortresses in the area, that's all. So, there aren't. Good. I'll make a note of it."

"'Tis a weird notion all the same," Arlette said suspiciously.

Loïc felt Diane hesitate, even retreat, before relaunching herself on the attack, her voice even shriller than before.

"And there's no seminary either? No cathedral town?"

Now the feeling of surprise reached its height: Arlette, who had the knife poised against the round loaf before cutting another slice – to everyone's consternation – stopped in mid-movement. Maurice began to laugh.

"No, we don't need no bishop nor no priest here. We don't have no time to say prayers, with all the work there is. Sundays the priest at Vignal comes to say mass. There was even a curate . . . once upon a time."

He stopped, then took up his story again, smiling.

"Even he left at a gallop, the little curate did. Isn't that right, Mother? He was very small, the curate they had. Couldn't always call on the Good Lord for help, poor man."

"That's enough, Maurice," Madame Memling said indulgently.

And Maurice said no more, but went on laughing. Loïc looked at him, then at Diane, like a game of tennis, until a noise in the corridor brought him out of this monotonous to-ing and fro-ing. The noise was followed by the arrival of Bruno, supported by Nochance. Bruno was bent double, his eyes feverish, and he banged himself on the door.

Nochance put him on the first chair he came to and drew up another to prevent him falling off, for with his heavy limbs he was involuntarily sliding to the floor.

The assembled company were for a moment flabbergasted, before suddenly coming to.

"What's you doing here, then?" Madame Memling shouted severely.

The accused rolled his eyes.

"Me, we so hungry. Nochance no leave him all alone."

"And why not? No one's going to steal him from you, you know," Diane, who'd come to her senses, cried. "You shouldn't be dragging him along corridors when he's riddled with fever, just because you're hungry. It's inhuman."

One could tell Diane had had *her* soup, Loïc thought prosaically. But, even so, she was right. He took up her point.

"She's right. Best leave him lying down . . . please. And he shouldn't be eating in his present state either. He must only drink."

"But me's had nothing," Nochance repeated, his face contorted with a conflict between passion and hunger, a conflict worthy of classical tragedy.

"Well, I'm going to put my friend to bed again.

110

You'd better not prevent me. Isn't that so, Loïc?" Diane said firmly.

She rose, and turned to go behind her chair, but not before whispering, "Take some cheese for me."

"Don't want to leave him," Nochance moaned. And slipping his monkeylike arms around Bruno's shoulders and knees, he wedged him further on to his chair.

"This has gone too far," Diane cried. "Leave him alone. Monsieur is Madame's fiancé, you must understand," she said pointing to Luce.

She felt red with rage but remained the epitome of dignity. But, as she turned to Luce, she saw that she had switched off and was miles away from this whole episode. Diane made a mental note and, as always when her convictions were not greeted with overwhelming approval, withdrew in a complete turnabout.

"Fine, then. To each his own. But as far as I am concerned, and since we're all in this together, Loïc, I hereby give notice that if I catch some sort of sunstroke, and Ghee-maw wants to drag me into his armchair, it will be contrary to my wishes, whatever he may claim. Can I count on you?"

As if called back to life by this simple possibility, the old man began to bray "Ghee-maw, ghee-maw " enthusiastically. Madame Memling turned to Nochance, and took away his two-seated nursing chair, or lovers' seat.

"Will you leave him alone?" she said dryly. "Go back to your room. First, you're not having any soup. No. What an idea . . . Soup. Why should you? Tomorrow, if you do some work, you can have soup. D'you think I'm going to feed you because you bring sick people

111

into my house? No. Now go. Take Monsieur back to his room, Meningou, or I'll put you outside."

Meningou looked towards the tureen, whimpered, and let Bruno go, who immediately fell off his chair to the floor, whereupon under the indignant gaze of his Parisian friends, Nochance picked him up, bundled him over his shoulder and went out through the door without even saying good night. There was silence at table, while Arlette gave each of them a piece of delicious, wonderful-smelling Brie. It was she who reestablished the atmosphere:

"No. Perhaps I should give him cheese as well!" she shouted indignantly. And everyone began to roar with laughter at this mad idea.

"Perhaps you thinks I'm a bit harsh, all the same," she went on with a dreamy look in her eye. "Refusing men bread. Which I did to your friend at midday."

Her Dostoevskian crisis was interrupted by a general outcry. A flood of proverbs such as: "He who merits nothing gets nothing", "The early bird catches the worm." "All hard work deserves a wage", etc. etc., intermingled with numerous "All he had to do was . . ." and "it's just that . . ." streamed from her guests' lips.

Relieved from their totally physiological anguish of hunger, and abandoning themselves a little to the delights of digestion, they now did their best to assuage their friend's touching scruples. So much so, that although they were all aware of the piece of Brie still left in the centre of the table, they never openly looked at it; however they did continue to watch it. And so each one of them attempted to wrest Arlette's

112

mind from her sterile remorse and lead her back to more amusing projects, projects closer to hand.

Nevertheless, the moral to be drawn from that day, its lesson, was revealed unambiguously to those city-dwellers: "Laziness was or should have been punished." Diane soon threw herself into a story, in the course of which John Rockefeller, having arrived late at the Stock Exchange, lost three quarters of his industrial empire. Luce continued by plaintively recalling a superb blue-white diamond that her husband had waited an hour at Cartier's for her to decide upon, and had finally refused her. The conversation lapsed, Loïc seemingly unable to remember any disastrous example of sloth. Already they could see Madame Memling poised to say the fatal "Good, well then. Everyone to bed," which would put an end to all hope of Brie, when at last Loïc took the initiative. He rose.

"Madame Henri . . . Arlette, sorry. Would you like me to go down and draw a little more wine from the barrel? Maurice showed me where it was this afternoon."

"True enough, 'tis thirsty times," said the aforementioned Maurice from where he was lolling in his chair, with blue bags under his eyes.

"'Tis very kind of you, Monsieur Loïc. Here, take the litre bottle. But wait for our little woman to rinse it for you."

And Luce Ader, the banker's wife, ran to the sink and the bottle-brush.

A little later, while Loïc was refilling their glasses with chilled wine, it was Diane who launched forth:

"You know, Arlette, this wine is exquisite. It's

113

delicious. So cool. And what a bouquet. It's a wine that appeals to the palate and not the throat. That's very rare."

"'Tisn't bad," Arlette conceded. "'Tisn't bad. A thirty-nine."

"And especially with cheese. It has an incredible bouquet. The one brings out the best in the other."

Arlette nodded in agreement, but made not the slightest move to verify it. A sort of hopelessness invaded Diane's heart. What was going to become of her in this house? Not only was she always hungry, not only did everything she ate seem to have an extravagant flavour, but, worse, this unhealthy obsession had over-whelmed all her friends as well (she felt Luce like Loïc ready to fight with their forks for their portions if she tried the least sleight of hand). Nevertheless, she could never be resigned.

"How will you make your tarts tomorrow, Arlette dear? Shortcrust or flaky? When I think that perhaps in three months' time, or perhaps even less, I'll be in Vienna, savouring the famous Sachertorte. Ah, those Germans, that man Hitler especially, that clown who thinks of himself in the Elysée Palace already. Ah no. Life. It makes you laugh, doesn't it?"

And, throwing her head back, her red hair, after twenty-four hours of rustic abandon, falling loose all over the place, she burst into sharp, convulsive laugh-ter, laughter such as might have come from the lips of Elizabeth I at Mary Stuart's execution (but which hardly explained the prospect of a chocolate torte, albeit from Sacher's). In full view of her anguished friends, Diane suddenly plunged her head on to her

114

left elbow, and while shaken by neurotic spasms of giggles, her right hand groped towards the cheese, which she pulled forward to her plate. The nearness of it increased her laughter, she did her head in both hands in modest refuge, out of which she emerged for one single moment, time enough to cut herself a large portion of cheese and toss it nonchalantly on to her plate. Holding her sides, and always maintaining the same absentminded expression, the same look of amused astonishment when faced with the vagaries of fate, she pushed the shrunken Brie back to the centre of the table. To emphasize the innocence of her behaviour and her absentmindedness, she tapped the handle of her knife for a good couple of minutes, time for her cascades of laughter slowly to subside and for her to reveal to her friends, her untidy make-up, her panting voice, and her triumphant eyes.

"Oh, sorry," she said to no one in particular in the group over which Madame Memling loured. "Sorry. I'm dead tired. I just don't know what I'm saying or doing any more. Oh my God, it's so good to have a laugh," she added cynically, as she coldbloodedly applied herself to her cheese, placing a good-sized chunk on a slice of bread she happened to have handy, and which, one might almost have thought, had been prepared in advance.

Reassured or hopping mad, they questioned the motive of her gaiety, to which she replied with much simpering, "Oh, nothing". Only Loïc could bring himself to comment truthfully, and he was flattering in his brevity.

"Well done," he said with such admiration that, of

Diane's double set of blushes, it was difficult to tell which was for greed, which for victory.

Madame Memling rose as though nothing had happened, nothing at least that might have registered with her. Each it seemed was making for their room, except Diane who recklessly lingered on, shaking hands three times each, first with young Maurice, then Luce, then Loïc, then Madame Memling, as though she had emerged from the vestry and was receiving the congratulations which were her due. She laughed, with a heady laugh, promising the mistress of the house she would help her with her entertaining the following day.

"And how many would there be for this lunch, Arlette dear?"

The conditional tense irritated Arlette who was absolutely relying on those who had promised to come.

"There'll be us, plus the Faberts, our neighbours, and their son, that make three, plus the Henri cousins, that make two more, perhaps three if they brings their workhand. With us that'll be fourteen, right? If there's thirteen, we'll bring Granfer to the table. Some people is superstitious about that," Madame Memling added, sniggering wildly, for some unknown reason.

Such a laugh froze the little group who were otherwise happy at the prospect of going to bed. But Diane quickly came to. Carried away by the sweet helium of her success and by affability, she floated like a scrawny hot-air balloon to her bedroom where she threw herself on the bed and began to snore without even having time to say goodnight to poor Luce. Although Luce was exhausted by the varied and overlong work, she had still to take off Diane's wine-coloured outfit, mined with press-studs. Throughout this undressing, Luce had to summon up every last drop of her kindness – or apathy – for a sort of inner squall had taken possession of her since the infamous raid on the cheese. And though she may have admired Diane's imagination and courage, she had appreciated far less the way she had subsequently shared her spoils, racked as she had been for the whole day by this unknown howling sensation which she did not know was hunger. That evening it was a wolf-bitch who'd been watching the Brie disappear down Diane's unique gullet. Be that as it may, she would have to wait until lunch the following day.

Feeling exhausted, hungry, fulfilled, Luce took off her clothes and slipped into the very small portion of bed Diane had left her: with its alternating rows of lumps it was hardly comfortable, but she too very swiftly fell asleep. For, gorgeous and delicious as life was at present, she could not make so much as the smallest plan for the future, no more than she could have when life was unpleasant. Luce was one of those women who lived from day to day, a species as rare in her sex as in the other.

As for Loïc, who could not bring himself to sleep with that strange couple, either on part of the bed-base or the mattress, he went and lay in the hay, as in the boy-scout stories he must have read as a boy, and of which he remembered absolutely nothing.

Chapter 7

Not a single cock-a-doodle-doo was heard from the Henris' rooster until just before breakfastime the following morning, which, Loïc thought, showed proof of a compassion and good sense rarely observed in domestic fowl. Everyone was gathered in the big room: in the Henri camp were Madame Memling – always true to form in her black apron – and her son Maurice in a brand-new vest and with his foot properly bandaged, and leaning on a gnarled stick; in the Paris camp were Diane Lessing, in a pair of black and white check dungarees over a severe black silk blouse, which would have made *any* harvester look overdressed. Luce had put on a girlish flowery blouse and a skirt with a fold-over panel which seemed as easy to undo as do up. Loïc himself had donned a superb blue and white striped shirt by Lacoste and a pair of navy-blue canvas trousers, intended for promenading on deck.

Hardly were they seated than the first arrivals, the Faberts, made their entrance. Ferdinand Fabert was a corpulent, straightforward sort of man, considered locally to be bad-tempered, but, according to Maurice, he wouldn't have hurt a fly. Whether this reputation was the cause or the effect, his face harboured a wild,

119

ferocious expression, which was emphasized even more by the fact that Josepha Fabert looked like a typical doormat.

"Hello there," they said in unison like two duettists perfectly in tune, and Loïc wanted to laugh, but confined himself to answering with "Hello there," and a nod as vigorous as theirs.

"Sit down, sit you down!" Arlette said. "You'll have a coffee first, won't you?"

"Ah! That!" Diane said, batting her eyelids like a young *in génue* and fixing her eyes on Ferdinand Fabert, who simply stared back at her, unblinkingly, like a wild animal. "Ah, yes. We're going to need a good coffee."

And she made a grand sweep of her arms to indicate the heat; it was meant to be a wide sweep, but in the event could only take in the small window and the door, which was currently closed. Everyone looked in the directions she was pointing, thinking to discover something annoyingly wrong, but finding nothing, looked away.

"Just in the time it took to get to you, Ferdinand's shirt got soaked through," Fabert's wife confirmed.

"I'm sure his shirt needs wringing out," Maurice chimed in. "With all the weight poor Ferdinand have to pull."

The four peasants burst out laughing and the slightly bewildered Parisians smiled inanely, not knowing quite why. But once Maurice's laughter had subsided, he enlightened them.

"The Faberts has a bike and a trailer. Ferdinand pedals in front and his fat wife sits behind," he said, pointing to the little bag of bones, hair and muscle that was Josepha Fabert, who smiled and shrugged her shoulders as if to play down her skinniness – just the opposite of what one would have done in Paris.

"It's good that it's not going to be very cold," Luce announced in a rare flash of imagination, which earned her a half-hearted look of approval from everyone.

"Isn't Nochance coming to work here today, then?" Josepha asked Arlette.

Although he'd suspected its existence, Loïc was amazed at the mysterious bush telegraph in the country, that could provide advance information on everyone else's business, and was every bit as successful as Reuters, but without transport, telegraph wires, or, it seemed, any sign of a messenger. Or could it be that grim-faced Madame Memling was beaming morse-code messages with her pocket torch every night to the whole of the Beauce, relaying her four Parisians' adventures and follies? Rather like a gigantic animated cartoon for farmers, with them as comic heroes.

Loïc smiled at this idea and, seeing him smiling, Arlette pointed him out importantly to the newcomers.

"This here is Monsieur Loïc . . . 'tis him who's looking after the harvesting at the moment," she said in a voice that threatened punishment if he were not respected. Leaving Loïc to understand that, with the help of his machine, he had achieved a status he could never have hoped for at the Quai d'Orsay. Certainly, he'd always had a gift for things mechanical, but he'd had so little occasion to test it . . .

"Next time one of my tractors is on the blink, I'll ask for you," Diane whispered into his ear.

121

She was obviously enchanted by the Faberts – her eyes sparkled. The least presence of strangers always excited her, and was a source of joy. Her taste for small talk was blossoming even on this farm. She became twice as ridiculously polite when the door opened again, and in filed a woman who looked amazingly like Arlette, but ten years younger, a stern-looking man who could have come from a Polytechnic, and a third, extremely shifty, totally antipathetic individual, who turned out to be a cousin of the unfortunate master of the house – currently detained behind barbed wire far from his farm.

"This here is my husband's cousin, Bayard Henri," Arlette said rapidly, her face tense. "And this here is my sister Odile Henri and their workhand Jojo."

The three people thus introduced sat down in a row on a bench and nodded their heads, studying the Parisians with eyes lowered. The oddest of them was cousin Bayard who never stopped sniggering, whether through shyness or pure nastiness, one couldn't tell. He was thirty, looked untrustworthy, and had tufts of hair sprouting at random, in unexpected places all over his body.

"Hello there," he said unnecessarily, and squinted salaciously at Luce's breasts, then quickly turned away, but continued to snigger, making everything seem twice as obscene.

"Allow me to introduce us now," Diane said with a smile.

She felt the very essence of good manners, of French courtesy. And she could already imagine how she would describe the scene to her friends later.

"I'll begin with myself, as one should. My name is Diane Lessing, I live in Paris, have no very definite profession, I admit" – and here she gave a small throaty laugh, making more hairs stand on end on Loîc's head and arms than he would have thought possible. But Diane was in full flood: "As for this young woman, this is Luce Ader, married to a brilliant Parisian businessman, who at this very moment is desperately waiting for us in Lisbon. I shall move on to Loïc Lhermitte, a top civil servant, a diplomat in fact, who's been looking after us since the beginning of our wanderings, to his great credit, I must admit. And finally, perhaps in a moment or two, I'll introduce you to our friend Bruno Delors, a wild young man, whose age excuses him. That's our little group."

There was a stunned silence, but unrebellious and undissenting, Loïc remarked with relief. The Beauce was a truly beautiful, peaceful, confident province, and, he told himself, he would remember it to the end of his days. Particularly when he saw Diane flash Arlette Henri a triumphant, affectionate, delighted wink, as if from the life-and-soul-of-the-party to the recently-anxious-mistress-of-the-house who, thanks to her efforts, was now reassured. The truth was of course that Madame Memling seemed not remotely concerned about the atmosphere of her party nor whether or not her guests were happy, and was far more interested in supplying them with a rake or a fork than a topic of conversation. She poured out more coffee for them, moving from bowl to bowl in a second round, which one gathered from her expression was certainly the final one.

123

"Good! So, who's going to fetch Meningou and . . . your friend?"

"Oh, but what on earth can be the matter, if they're not even up yet, at this hour?" Arlette's double exclaimed, looking indignantly at the clock, which pointed to almost 7.45 a.m.

At this, Loïc's mind was set in motion: he was flooded by fond memories of a lazy, party-going man, who adored night life, a man who for the last twenty-four hours had accepted the customs and maxims of the Henri family as docilely as he had once accepted those of the Faucigny-Lucinges.

"Bruno . . . our friend got sunstroke very badly yesterday when he was out walking," Luce whined in protest.

"'Tis true your friend did look a bit peeky yesterday," Maurice confirmed.

Luce glanced at him in tender reproach. Bayard Henri intercepted that glance between them and immediately jumped to a thousand conclusions – all of which were correct. That forced him to unfreeze his rictus to the extent of exposing his upper canines, which were very yellow and protruded, and which, in Diane's eyes, made him utterly repulsive. According to Diane, a minimum of attractiveness should be expected from every human being mixing in society. (This was the type of maxim Diane would make her debating point, should it happen to be introduced into the conversation.) Like everyone else, she felt an active antipathy towards Bayard Henri but, instead of defending her views about him, she revelled in them as an expression of her very reliable instinct: her flair.

She sidled towards Arlette who was carefully putting away her bread, cups and *cafetière* in the sideboard, in order to say to her:

"I hope you haven't teamed me up with your cousin Bayard."

Arlette glanced at her, surprised, opened her mouth to say something, but Ferdinand who had been sent off to find the missing persons, reentered the room, literally carrying Bruno under his left arm and dragging Nochance by the scruff of his neck with his right.

"He don't look as though he's ready for reaping, this one," he said, dropping poor Bruno on to his usual chair (from which he began to slide, as on the previous day), but mercifully, Loïc caught him and propped him against the table. Bruno was a pale green colour, and was sweating large drops of sweat, his eyes wandering, totally lost.

"This is a gradual sunstroke – one that comes in stages", Diane announced, in a decisive, educated voice which caught everyone's attention.

"What's that?" several voices demanded.

"A gradual sunstroke is one which feeds on itself, and can last three, four, or five days. It's a Moroccan expression. My second husband and I learnt it from the Sultan of Fez, one spring when he'd invited us to stay with him. The poor man caught this sunstroke and had to spend three weeks in hospital – in *his* hospital I should say – while we stayed on in his palace.

"What luxury those Arabs live in!" she confided in hushed tones to Josepha, seated next to her. "It was perhaps a little ostentatious, rather over the top, but superb even so. Say what you like," she added.

125

Unfortunately Josepha didn't say anything to Diane of what she thought of Arab luxury, for Arlette dryly butted in: "Yes, but while we're waiting, this gradual sunstroke isn't at all convenient to me."

Loïc, Diane and Luce looked hurt and guilty (which was exactly what they were feeling since, as responsible people, people of conviction, they were also officially responsible for Bruno's illness, now that they knew the gravity and importance of their respective roles.)

"Good," Ferdinand said authoritatively. "Good, so the men will have to make do with four. Two can be down below pitching the trusses on to the wagons, and two on top to stack them. Then we can change over every so often, two below, two on top, to save our backs. Agreed? Arlette and Madame Diane," he said nodding to them, "can take care of the cooking. That still have to be done. All the other women have to do is follow on behind us, and rake up any wheat we've missed." At that point, he turned away (since there were women present) and spat a long stream of brownish saliva on to the floor behind him.

"Which fields still has to be harvested?" he then asked Loïc, professional to professional.

Loïc had adopted a truly idiotic, self-satisfied expression, Diane noted in passing.

"I've done the three fields, over there, which border the track, and I've begun the fourth near the dip. I had a bad time, there were so many small stones everywhere."

The poor man was stammering about it.

"So, you has only to finish that while we picks up the first ones," Ferdinand said.

And with no malice intended, he said, "Come on then, you daft bunch, let's be on our way."

"I'm coming with you all the same," Maurice said. "I can manage the horses, at least, and also show Mademoiselle Luce . . . how to do the gleaning."

He looked so unhappy and humiliated by his temporary infirmity that Loïc gave him a compassionate smile, which, to his great surprise, Maurice gratefully returned. Quite suddenly he seemed no more than a child, and Loïc was once more susceptible to his charm.

"I suppose no one has a camera," Diane asked with a smile. "Because no one in Paris will ever believe us. Luce a gleaner and Loïc on the combine-harvester. Oh, we need some proof, we really do."

And when no one responded, she added, sweetly and gently: "It needn't be a Leica. Just a box camera would do." But it seemed no one in the Beauce liked taking photos, for no one replied.

Thereupon, everyone stood up and made for the door; outside, even as early as eight in the morning, the heat was already aggressive. But Nochance's breaking voice put a stop to the general exodus.

"No! Nochance no going to fields. No leaving her alone with him."

Nochance's voice had that disturbing shrillness and ability to carry that simple people have, qualities which diminish with age as well as with insanity, and this, combined with Nochance's thwarted passion, managed to upset everyone.

All but Ferdinand half-turned, and gaped at him, astounded, as he pointed an accusing finger at Diane Lessing, who was also astounded (but not for long).

"Won't, won't, I tell you. Won't. You see how she looks at him."

"But . . . Isn't there nothing he won't invent!" Arlette Henri exclaimed indignantly.

"The boy's raving mad," Loïc said amused.

"Oh really. Someone's got to shut him up. He's a liar," Luce went one better.

"But . . . but . . . honestly. Am I dreaming, Luce my dear, tell me I'm dreaming?"

Diane's doleful, timid voice, which was intended to make the harvesters admire Parisian self-control and forbearing, made Loïc and Luce cringe, for they instantly recognized it as the prelude to a tornado. Both ducked and exchanged encouraging looks.

"Am I dreaming? Or has this boy accused me of evil intentions towards this poor young man, Bruno, whom I've known, along with his mother, for more than twenty years?"

"Makes no difference. Not leaving him with you," Nochance said stubbornly.

"Oh, try to see reason, monsieur. Certainly, if I were twenty, you'd be right not to leave me alone with M. Bruno Delors. He's the most handsome boy in Paris, he's appreciated for that by all the women in the capital; they're all fighting for his services, but he has never, never looked at another boy."

"But," Nochance blustered, all red in the face, "but . . ."

"And it would need someone as depraved and brawny as you to take advantage of his sunstroke. He must have thought you were a woman. That's the only explanation."

128

Faced with their incredulous, fascinated and slightly shocked expressions on learning Bruno's stated profession, and with Loïc's open hilarity, she put everyone in the picture. "It's true it needed an incredibly severe attack of sunstroke for him to see you as a member of the weaker sex, I admit. But if that's not the case, it means that you forced him. Yes, monsieur. Forced. I don't know what your reputation is locally, but it does not seem to be beyond reproach. Am I wrong?" she asked brusquely, turning to Arlette, who jumped. She had been fascinated by Diane's rhythmic voice, its notes of anger and sincerity as she held forth in her check dungarees, which looked for all the world like a Roman toga. It was better than the wireless.

But she could say or do nothing except be astonished. The idea of Nochance behaving evilly with this very vain, arrogant young man? She turned to him.

"Meningou. Did you do things to Monsieur?"

"Things?"

"Yes, things. Don't play the giddy goat with me. Things like you did to the curate?"

"What curate?" Diane exclaimed, enchanted by his titillating past.

Loïc signalled to her to keep quiet. Meningou had stood up; his eyes were round, his cheeks red.

"Done nothing to Monsieur Bruno. First didn't want to. And then me neither. And then he wanted give me everything he got. I refused everything. Even wanted give me goats and dates and I said no to everything he wanted to give me . . . so there . . .."

"Everything except his watch," Arlette said severely.

129

"Yes, except watch. But me no like dates very much," the accused said in self-justification.

Arlette turned to Diane. She seemed relieved by the explanation but disappointed by the time they had lost. The harvesters brightened up, recalled their duty and once more made for the door.

"Good," Arlette said to Meningou. "You heard what the lady said. She have absolutely no designs on your friend. Now leave her in peace and go to work. Go on. Go."

And, on the verge of tears, Meningou followed them, muttering incomprehensible things.

"But who told you he doesn't lie?" Diane asked Arlette once they had put poor Bruno, who looked increasingly like a puppet and a dog-tired puppet at that, back to bed, with a lime tisane, and they had begun to peel a vegetable unknown to Diane, and in her opinion it could have remained so.

"Meningou," Arlette said, "never lies. He's incapable of lying, poor boy."

She had uttered these words calmly, as if she were presenting a classic case history in psychiatry as well as describing a sad illness.

"Who was the curate?"

"A little student from the seminary. He were very timid, poor boy. Very sad too. The priest didn't know how to console him."

"Console him for what?"

"Nochance . . . um . . . stabbed him. It were a stormy day. He always get upset when there's a storm; you has to keep children and young people out of his way. The rest of the time he's . . . calm. You're peeling those far

130

too thick, Madame Diane," Arlette said. "There'll be nothing left of my courgettes."

"Courgettes? Are these courgettes? I've never seen any raw like this, they're really funny."

"And how've you seen them, then? Haven't you never seen them before?"

"No, to be honest, I've only ever seen them in a gratin before."

"Well, today you'll see them in a gratin as well; but first you sees them raw. There's always something to learn, my dear lady, as you can see."

"Yes indeed, indeed," Diane said with scarcely veiled melancholy.

After being frightened by her, she was now beginning to feel genuine affection for Arlette Henri. (How unsuitable her first name was). She would have loved to have a friend like her in Paris, someone "straight", she thought of the English word, as she did every time there seemed no appropriate word in French and she was with someone who spoke English sufficiently well to appreciate her bilingualism: otherwise, if she couldn't think of a word and was alone, she'd just forget about it, she thought with remorse. That was what was good about the country, there was time to have little conversations with oneself; it was quite funny, and certainly good for the mind. Very healthy. When she was back in Paris, she'd try to continue doing it. In Paris or New York, my God, they didn't even know which capital they'd be in in a week's time, they could be five or ten thousand kilometres from France, or in prison perhaps. And there she was, marvelling about the Beauce. André. André Ader. They absolutely had

131

to get in touch with André Ader. Tell him they were alive, and not to go off on his ship and leave them on some farm or other, with almost no money (she would never sell her jewels in an emergency. That she'd sworn to each of the people – husbands and the rare lovers – who'd given them to her. She'd also sworn it to herself. It was too stupid to sell jewels when you were hard-pressed; you only got a quarter of their value when you had to sell them to the lowest bidder. Whether it was jewels and the rest or furs. And why sell your jewels at all if it wasn't an emergency? In short, one had to ensure one never found oneself in an emergency, and that was that.)

"D'you really think I ought to put the vegetables on a separate dish from the chickens? Would it look better?"

Arlette looked anxious. The refinements Diane had suggested had gradually convinced her, and she was making a conscious effort to do everything better, which Diane found quite touching.

Diane's voice was very decisive, a voice that would make chickens run for cover.

"Yes, of course you must. And you must divide up the four chickens according to their joints as well, with the white meat on one side, the dark on the other. So that way people can eat what they want to for once, without being disappointed."

Arlette nodded. If you used logic, you could make Arlette do whatever you wanted even in her own home. You could even transform it into a hunting lodge or a brothel.

Diane was delighted to act as guide.

132

"Tell me, Arlette, excuse me for asking, but have you lost all your hair? Did it happen a long time ago?"

"What on earth d'you mean? 'Tis all here."

Madame Memling looked rattled, which made her much more human.

"How should I know when you're always wearing a headscarf? Show me if it's true?" Diane said laughingly.

Ten minutes later, Arlette had her hair in a chignon and was wearing lip gloss: she had also unbuttoned her dress a little at the neck. These three details made a woman of her, Diane thought, feeling well pleased with her skills and quite moved by her own kindness. It was a pity Arlette had refused all garments Diane had offered to lend her. The Balenciaga costume was very plain and would have suited her admirably, but she had even been inflexible about a pair of trousers in autumn colours and a suede jacket which had a "field sports look" and a very "simple" cut.

However, Arlette did not allow closer acquaintanceship to stand in her way. An hour later, she sent her Pygmalion off to feed the animals.

Diane set out with four billy-cans, stumbling along in her high-heeled kid bootees.

While everything may have gone well with the poultry, she did encounter some difficulties with the pigs who were waiting by their trough for her, grunting behind a low door. Diane had to lean over it to pour the meal – a mixture of bran and water – between them, but they were all jammed up so tight around her it was quite impossible.

She decided to put their tin on the ground, open the

door and slide it in between them with her foot. Except that, as soon as she put the dish through, a piglet, which was livelier than the rest, launched itself through the half-open door, seemingly more interested in freedom than food. Diane found it really rather fun two or three times, and, always conscious of her imaginary public behind her, even shouted "Will you please stop that . . . you little devil" when she was at her most amused. But when, at the fourth attempt, she was literally butted and found herself sitting on the ground in her check dungarees while the piglet and his brothers and sisters attempted to escape over the top of her, she began to scream in despair: piercing cries of distress rather than command, which fortunately frightened the animal into returning to its siblings, who were already at table.

With her brow soaked in sweat and legs trembling, her dungarees covered in stains, but standing upright, Diane went to her room to change. As she took off her ruined attire, she finally began to wonder whether or not she had been fortunate in finding this farm? They had escaped gunfire, in this unending exodus, perhaps they would never have done more than five kilometres more up till now, but perhaps all her compatriots had reached where they wanted to go? Perhaps they themselves would have been near Lisbon by now? How could one know? Diane thought that, by divine right, all the hazards had been hazards which had been useful to her, but now, after the piglet episode, she had lost much of her arrogance and much of her optimism as well.

And who could she rely on now, out of Loïc who was absorbed in his mechanical engineering and Luce who spent her time flirting with the young farmer? Neither of them seemed particularly keen to leave. Only she was. She and poor Bruno who had perhaps escaped a shameful rape but not raging sunstroke. Would he remain gaga for long? In the meantime, she had to banish her sad thoughts, and go and help Arlette with their lunch for fourteen. All through her life, she had managed to hold any serious anxieties at bay by plunging herself into the social whirl, or losing herself in obligations which forced her to sacrifice herself. And just as well, she thought.

Chapter 8

Arlette was so immersed in her cooking that she'd given no thought to laying the table. But Diane was keeping an eye open for any problems, and had gone to great lengths in her refinement, even putting little name cards in front of each place setting. Presiding over the table was the mistress of the house and her son Maurice, seated between Luce and Diane, while next to Arlette was Loïc on one side, while Bruno would have been on the other, had he been in better health. His place was taken by cousin Bayard, since Diane had chosen the powerful and disturbing Ferdinand to sit next to herself. As there were five women and seven men, she had coldly put the two least talkative and least brilliant of the assembled company, Nochance and the farmhand nicknamed Jojo, together. As she wrote "Jojo" on his name card, Diane laughed, albeit modestly. In Parisian society, there was a Yeye, and a Zouzou – but of course it had to be said they were Yeye de Montague and Zouzou Prélevant. And, naturally, Paris was Paris.

The harvesters returned on the dot at midday, red-faced, sweating, bent double, and shattered. They had to be revived with water or watered-down wine for a good ten minutes before they could speak. Then they sat at table. And the beginning of the meal was so silent that it put Diane in mind of a recent, uncomfortable wedding.

Lunch began with an enormous slice of pâté and dried sausage: real stodge, Diane thought, but Arlette had not heeded her suggestion of shredded carrot and raw artichoke, which would also have been very "easy to prepare". Diane therefore did like everyone else and helped herself to a large serving.

"These cold meats are delicious," she said in a head voice, in the exhausted silence, broken only by the noise of cutlery and, more unpleasantly, by munching. "Do you prepare them yourself?"

"Of course we prepares everything from the pig ourselves!" Ferdinand cried, as he gradually returned to life. "Do you have pâté like this where you comes from, dear lady?"

"Well no. I have to admit. Isn't that so, Loïc? Can you ever recall a terrine as exquisite as this?"

"Definitely not," Loïc said. "It's very, very good. Very . . ." He gave up on his adjectives and wolfed down his portion with the same speed – if not the same noise – as his workmates. This was the same Loïc Lhermitte, who in Paris would balk at any dish cooked in a sauce.

"And when does the execution take place . . . I mean when is the poor pig killed?"

"Come October. You must come back for it," Ferdinand said, brimming with Beauceron hospitality. "You'll see, fresh black pudding, and that's not the half of it. The blood you sees pouring from the pig in the morning, you eats grilled at mid-day."

Diane had turned a ghastly shade of pale.

"My God." she said. "Well . . . well . . . that must be . . . cheering."

"And there's the offal too. What we do call the guts, 'tisn't the same word as with you – but there, you really has to see it for yourself. We puts the guts directly into the . . ."

The description of the pig and its entrails almost got the better of Diane. Happily, the poultry arrived on the table and the conversation turned to that: a dish whose charms and internal organs were less spectacular in their portrayal.

"If you find any feathers, it won't be my fault," Diane warned.

"'Twasn't you that had to pluck them, was it?"

"No, absolutely not. But Mem . . . Arlette I mean, wanted me to do it. I was terrified. How d'you tear the feathers out of those poor little creatures? It's like pulling hairs out one by one."

"Well, 'tis like this: if I was dead, I wouldn't give a toss," Ferdinand declared. "You don't pluck them alive. But I'll bet you don't know how to kill them either? I'll show you if you likes."

And Ferdinand bent down and scooped up one of the fowl wandering around Diane's feet. Diane was no longer astonished, but she stared wide-eyed and horrified as he laid the squawking, struggling bird in front of them.

"You takes them by the neck, like this here, and . . . snap . . ."

139

"Oh no! no!" Diane cried. "No! No, please don't. Poor creature. You're killing my appetite. Please monsieur."

"Call me Ferdinand then."

"Please, dear Ferdinand," Diane simpered, but her voice was quavering.

"You leave my chickens alone, you great pillock!" Arlette shouted.

With a wink, Ferdinand threw the miraculously recovered hen into the air, and it skimmed past Luce, who let out piercing screams.

"Well then, I'm thinking 'twould be better if you came after the pig's slaughtered," Ferdinand deduced. "It screams its head off, it do. You can't hear nothing else for a whole kilometre or more, for ten minutes, isn't that right, Maurice?"

"Oh, when it come to screaming, it really scream," he confirmed with his dreamy eyes and his leg wedged between Luce's.

"And so," Diane said in her serious voice, "there must be a sort of . . . violence, must there, in agricultural life, of which we're absolutely unaware in the city?"

"In the city, you spends your time running over people in your cars. There isn't no pigs to bleed, but there's pedestrians."

The remark came from the permanently repellent cousin Bayard, who was now fancying himself as a globetrotter.

"You have a very pessimistic notion of traffic," Diane said dryly. "The dangers are minimal."

"Ah, well yes. I went to your Paris once, not so long

140

ago, and four times I was nearly killed. I seed a woman flattened in the street. With my own eyes, I seed her. At the Eiffel Tower 'twas."

"That's bad luck," Diane said. "I can assure you . . ."

"But I seed what I seed," said the nasty cousin. "And not only was she runned over, the poor woman, but there was dozens of cars, end to end, you couldn't move, I had to walk all the way back to where I was staying. 'Twas a fair step, I can tell you."

There was a silence. Loïc was ready to boast the charms of Paris even so, but the sight of Diane's flushed face dissuaded him from adding anything to the discussion. She said:

"Well, all I can say to reassure you, dear monsieur, since you only see what you want to see, is that you witnessed a suicide and a traffic jam, full stop. And if that is all you managed to see in our capital, then you have just cause for complaint."

Delighted with her remark, she turned away peremptorily and pretended to be interested in what the visionary, Bruno's lover, was trying to say. For the last five minutes he'd been desperately tugging at her sleeve.

"What is it now?" she asked, a victorious gleam in her eye.

"If you no want, why no give to me?" the boy asked.

Clearly, the boy was obsessed.

"You are completely . . . you've become overheated in the sun," she caught herself saying before she saw Loïc looking at her severely. Which reminded her just in time that one must never talk about madness to madmen; it was the kind of advice you're generally given confidentially and sternly, as if, left to your own devices, you'd talk about callouses to an amputee, lungs to a TB sufferer, or Frankenstein's monster to someone truly ugly.

Even so, poor Bruno had made rather more brilliant conquests in Paris in his time . . . Would he recover from this awful gradual sunstroke? It would be great fun arriving in New York with a raving nutcase on one's arm. On ones arm? More likely holding his hand, taking him back to his mother, judging by the state he was in now. Of course, one could say it had been an accident, a cracked skull, a German bullet which he'd got when he was harrying a hostile Stuka . . . but in the end heroism didn't excuse lethargy.

"Why don't you give your pâté to that boy, since you isn't eating it," Ferdinand said. Then he turned to Arlette:

"Madame Diane finds her pâté so good, she don't want to give it to no one. Look, I likes it when a woman takes a good forkful," he said giddily, seeing the skeletal state of his neighbour and his wife.

Or was it the gesture he liked? Loïc wondered. Diane blushed at her error but, fortified by red wine, she once more took up her role of sociologist, and asked her moustachioed neighbour, Ferdinand, what he managed to do on winter evenings when the snow and wintry weather prevented work in the fields.

"Don't you get bored in the evening, when it gets dark by about six? Don't you feel a little melancholy?"

No, Ferdinand did not feel melancholic, it seemed. He laughed instead and looked at her.

"Well no, you know. First of all everything have to be put in order. Everything that've been broken in the summer, harness, tools, and then for those that has the luck to have a really hot little number like you in their bed, winter don't seem long at all . . . it passes quick even."

Diane blinked, put down her knife and fork and gave a little strangled laugh. Let it be understood, she had received many different compliments in the course of her life. People had praised her elegance, her class, her race, her mind, even her charm, but it was actually the first time a man had described her as "a really hot little number". She was astonished, and in all honesty, enchanted. That she should hear this compliment from the lips of this somewhat simple countryman was very, very astonishing, for it had to be said that his sense of light-hearted gallantry, his polite sensuality was completely innate. No one could say that this man had learnt good manners from anyone. The only annoying thing about this compliment was that there was absolutely no way she could ever repeat it to anyone. She imagined Loïc's response if she spoke about herself as "a really hot little number" to him. Even Loïc, however discreet he was, would be unable to resist repeating it. She didn't dare think about what would happen in Paris . . .

At this point, Arlette brought in the tarts. Out of the four, three were exquisite, and one inedible; this one, it seemed, contained all the bitter apples from the three crates. How could that have happened? It was a question which haunted poor Diane's mind for most of that night and the following day: because, in the end, she'd thrown them all together, higgledy-piggledy, into the same pot. It was unbelievable. When Loïc was consulted, he replied somewhat absentmindedly that he was "buggered" if he knew how. He was beginning to pick up a farmyard vocabulary, which would not go down well in New York or in Paris, or God knows where they'd end up. But how could the apples have . . .?

To end this immense lunch, Arlette, imprudently, at Ferdinand's behest, had the homemade Plum passed round. And after "hesitating" for some time, and remembering that this liqueur had impaired her gait and her mind once before, Diane accepted a small glass. It seemed it was much weaker than on the first occasion but, doubtless, Ferdinand's encouragement helped her.

All the same, Diane must have abused this excellent, wholesome Plum brandy a little, since, shortly afterwards, she discovered she was singing, her arms linked with her neighbours, "Cock-eyed Nini", with her new "peasant family", as she referred to them. As some nightclub managers in Paris or Monaco still recall, she had a raucous voice, which, when she was slightly tipsy, became incredibly powerful. Had she used this same vocal organ the other day in the cart, a passing Wagnerian might have mistaken her for one of the Walkyrie haranguing her messengers: a simultaneously terrifying and anachronistic vision. But here she was, under Loïc's astonished, delighted gaze, and the less thrilled but nonetheless admiring eyes of Luce (who was becoming more and more distracted), singing away at "The Tarts of Camaret" and other jolly songs.

At this juncture, Arlette spirited away the bottle of Plum, and cast eloquent glances towards Ferdinand, who rose, wiping his mouth with his hand, with a naturalness Diane found adorable.

"Come on, then," he cried. "When you has to go, you has to go."

At last the harvesters set off, but not without Ferdinand attempting to fondle Diane's behind as he passed. Of rather he fondled what he thought had been there all his life, and appeared more bemused than disappointed by the experience: Diane herself was half-indignant, half-captivated, and for a long time she watched his robust figure disappearing into the distance, with Luce and Loïc hobbling along behind him.

During their lunch the harvesters had awakened Bruno from his long sunstroke. For a moment he stayed with his eyes closed listening to "Cock-eyed Nini" – a choir led by a shrill, powerful woman's voice, a virago's voice in fact, which every now and then had a little of the same timbre as Diane Lessing's. Poor Diane. Imagine her at a country banquet. He smiled. Then he noticed his case open on the floor with his polo necks and shirts spilling out. So he must have got back? But how? He'd set out on a mission to find some sort of civilization, or at least somewhere to send a telegram from, and he'd failed. It was unbelievable. Bruno fell asleep again and awoke for a second time three hours later. Once more, he'd been tormented by the same dream: he'd never had a dream so intimate and so realistic, or one which he'd remembered so well. He recalled the exotic quality of his nightmare, the interminable sand, the nape of a Tuareg's neck, and, especially, being dragged down corridor after corridor, and ending up on the floor by a table where everyone was laughing most cruelly. He could still feel his shame as he slid to kneel before these emirs and their harem, whose faces were indistinguishable. He sighed. And then there was this sort of smell, the smell of that sweating slave who was carrying him, which still seemed to be lingering in his room . . . which was in fact in his room. Bruno sat up and opened his eyes properly. Sitting at the foot of his bed was an indescribable individual whose eyes were the emptiest he had ever seen. It really was an idiot, some sort of primate who was staring at him, fixedly.

"You better? You awake?"

So, this moronic creature talked like an African native. Léon Blum's much-vaunted scheme for educating rural areas had obviously been of little use. And Bruno who was the least socialist in the world could already see himself making ironic comments about it at parties in Paris, or New York.

"I beg your pardon?" he said. "Who are you?"

"Nochance."

"I'm not asking you for anything . . ." He stopped. It would be better to be conciliatory towards this bizarre personage.

Was he one of the Henri sons? No, even the army wouldn't take on such a specimen. He sat on his bed, and noted gratefully that he was wearing his underpants, for the other person was looking at him in a disturbing way . . . . No, not in a sexual way, of course: that would be wide of the mark as far as this unfortunate person was concerned – he'd probably never even held a girl's hand. Bruno felt overwhelmed by the man, who was almost freakish in his ugliness and, pointing with his forefinger to his own chest, said:

"Me, Bruno. Me, Bruno." Then, pointing with his finger to the other person's chest, he asked:

"And you, your name is?"

"Nochance," the other repeated irritatedly, which was the last straw.

Bruno shrugged his shoulders and half-lay on the bed. He felt weak.

"Where my friends?" he asked.

"Your friends at harvest."

"At harvest? Poor sods."

For a moment he imagined Luce with a scythe, then Loïc on his machine – which was already even better. And finally, Diane with a scythe: the vision seemed so apocalyptic to him that he immediately banished it from his mind. Diane with a scythe, felling all before her: countryside, trees, men, dogs, cats, hens! He couldn't help laughing.

"My friends happy?"

"Your friends happy when me bring you back."

"Because you bring me back?"

So, he was his saviour as well. He must have found him unconscious and brought him back on one of the broken-down carts, which were beginning to play an increasingly important role in Bruno's life.

"Me compensate you? Me give you . . .?"

"No dates. Me no like dates."

Bruno was indignant:

"Why should I give you dates?"

"Dates and goats."

Bruno was dumbfounded. What's more, this brute seemed to mean what he was saying.

"But no. Me pay you. With money."

"Me refused your watch, too," the other replied with a somewhat pious expression.

Bruno felt a surge of respect for this gorilla, who had brought him back to port instead of robbing him blind.

"You good bugger!" he said.

And leaning over, he patted the stranger on the shoulder. Immediately the man knelt at the foot of the bed and leant his face towards him fervently.

"You kiss me."

Bruno leapt back, but too late. The door had opened and Diane was watching them from the doorway. Leaning against the doorpost, she had adopted an almost enticing pose, as though she were soliciting, which startled him at first, then made him angry.

"Am I disturbing you?" she asked pointedly.

"Oh please Diane, don't be grotesque. What on earth's been happening to me?"

Diane began to laugh.

"What happened is that you were brought back from your escapade suffering from sunstroke, by this young man here, and we don't know, given his eclectic tastes, if you had access to the same favours as the members of his flock or the local curate. And that's it."

Bruno cast a horrified, incredulous glance at his suitor who was no longer on his knees, thank God, then at Diane.

"So Bruno, you're beginning to enjoy the country-side?"

That was Loïc; it was exactly the sort of quip Loïc would make. He had arrived behind Diane, and was leaning against the other doorpost, smiling, tanned, virile (he had to admit), and irritating.

"Loïc, was it you who . . . don't tell me . . . what Diane's been telling me, it must be crazy, I mean, about . . ."

With his chin, he indicated the savage, who still wore his perpetual angelic smile.

Loïc adopted a reassuring tone of voice:

"No, old man, we know absolutely nothing about it. All we know is that Nochance . . . has rather mixed tastes . . . But from there to say that you are no longer as you were when you left . . ."

Diane began to laugh and Bruno wanted to remonstrate with her, but stopped. She had just expelled a loud, drunken hiccup which in polite society one responded to with a stony face and a flood of words, as to all imponderable situations of this kind. Only instead of casting an accusing glance at her neighbours, as contrite hiccuppers generally did, Diane did something unreal: she opened the straw bag she had on her arm, inspected it inside in a bemused sort of way, and snapped it shut. Loïc and Bruno were taken aback for a moment, then Bruno saw the urge to laugh reddening Loïc's sunburnt cheeks, but not for long. Loïc had just come back from the fields after Nochance's abrupt departure, for he'd run back as soon as he'd finished his half hectare. Loïc was dead tired and no longer had his customary clearheadedness. The conversation between Diane and Bruno had suddenly seemed like a surrealist dream, an irrelevance. He reckoned, with some amusement, that, this evening in any case, only the harvesters would be entitled to any respect from him. Anyone else, whoever they were, even if by a miracle they arrived in a Rolls from the Academy of Sciences, would seem like wimps lost in abstraction to him. Despite her drunkenness, Diane at least had helped make the apple tarts and sampled the cold meats, which made her a relatively more wholesome person than Bruno with his third-degree sunstroke. Loïc was one up on Luce's husband with all his invisible millions. Loïc had touched ground, returned to the soil, plucked wheat – the source of bread no less – from the earth. He began to laugh about himself; about himself and parties he'd gone to, the life he'd led, and for that matter the life he would continue to lead. Just as in a few days' time he'd be laughing about his life as a farmer, as, in any case, it was something to laugh about when your name was Loïc Lhermitte, and you were past fifty, and could see that the life you had led had not been absolutely obligatory. When you could see that certain unbearable moments in the past should, in fact, have been unbearable, and simply that; and that certain moments of happiness, which were slightly dubious at the time, were, with hindsight, precisely that. In short, you could see that "ruining your life" was not just an expression found in novels.

"I think he's going to bite me." Diane said.

She had been sitting on the other side of the bed, facing Bruno, who was still lying down, and Nochance was indeed giving her savage looks: you could almost see him drawing back his lips in a snarl, and exposing his teeth – which were like an old dog's. She turned to Loïc. (Dear Diane really was a bit drunk.)

"I think this boy thinks I'm about to throw myself on Bruno, doubtless with him joining in. As if I could do that under this very roof," she said, waving extravagantly at the fly-blown ceiling. "And as if I'm going to show an innocent boy like him all my tricks and perversions: he'd be every bit as incapable of forgetting them, as he'd be of teaching his sheep how to do them."

Loïc was seized by the giggles, followed by Diane. It was exhaustion, the total break from routine, the bizarreness of their adventure, the complete change. It was goodness knows what, but they were literally convulsed and Diane had to get up and totter over to the wall. Strange, thought Loïc. It was strange to see human beings as different as Diane and himself sharing the same laughter; there was something mysterious, illogical and powerful in their giggling, something in the psychological jigsaw of a person that would occasionally explode, and could not be reconciled with the rest of their character, but was as important to share as sensual pleasure. Diane and he, for example, had nothing in common except parties, but they had the same, sometimes almost ridiculous kind of laughter, always about the same things, laughter that grabbed you, swept you along, made you distraught, doubled you up, laughter which, if it was missing from a couple, even a passionate couple, would mean a flaw in their relationship at a vital moment. And just as a lack of this laughter could explain apparently needless separations, so its presence could explain love affairs between completely ill-matched couples, for at that very moment, no one could have come between Loïc and Diane. But eventually they calmed down, and sat carefully, one on a chair, the other on the windowsill, like two people with terrible wounds struggling to survive, which is how victims of uncontrollable laughter behave afterwards. They each glanced at the other to check that they had returned to normal and their attack had subsided, then both reverted to their usual state of suspicion, aggravation, mutual indifference, in short, to their dual solitude. Only then could they go back to Bruno's bedside.

Bruno had adopted an expression which they both knew by heart and which was his version of incomprehension – an indulgent eye under a raised eyebrow, and lip-biting – the whole face indicating a sort of amused condescension. Unfortunately, as they now saw, Nochance was beginning to emulate him adoringly. Placed where he was, Bruno couldn't see him. In any case, since he'd reverted to his usual narcissism, he didn't even think to look at his imitator. Nochance had raised his eyebrows up to his hairline – his forehead was relatively low – and his eyes were creased up so tightly they had practically disappeared; he wasn't biting his huge lower lip, he was almost chewing it. It took a moment for Loïc and Diane to understand what this strange mimicry was attempting to convey. But at the very moment they grasped its meaning. Bruno, who continued to fix them with his impassive stare, stretched his arms, and nonchalantly flicked his cigarette ash on to dear Arlette's tiled floor. Then, without even looking, Nochance also held out his great beefy hand

152

and by chance his fag-end too, and also flicked the ash and cinders on to the heap of Bruno's pullovers inadvertently within his reach.

"Am I to be allowed to know what's going on?" Bruno asked haughtily.

And as if to show how tired he was, he stretched out his hand again, and heedlessly stubbed his cigarette on the floor. Nochance, his eyes always half closed, did the same, and it was only as it went through the third pullover that he must have realized something was amiss. After glancing furtively at these strange jumpers, he hurriedly withdrew his hand, and swung it back between his knees. It needed nothing more for Loïc and Diane to plunge back into hysterical laughter. They set off towards the door, bumping into one another, and only Loïc managed the presence of mind to murmur some inaudible excuses on the way.

With his two friends gone, Bruno turned to Nochance, who had a peculiar expression on his face, like someone who'd swallowed a particularly corrosive chilli and who, with eyes closed, would also like to swallow his chin.

"Go and fetch me some water," he said to him.

After all, if he had to put up with this strange admirer, he might as well make use of him, as his valet. There were quite a few intelligent men around who had moronic valets. Wasn't one of them Don Juan? Perhaps not. Or wasn't there someone in one of Molière's plays? He couldn't recall who (it must be said that Bruno's erudition was fairly limited, confined as it had been to between 1900 and 1930). He decided to put on one of his pullovers and a striped pair of trousers – his "yachting" gear, but so what? – he hadn't foreseen he'd

153

need farm clothes when he'd assembled his wardrobe. He laughed lightly and looked at himself in the mirror, the pathetic little glass hanging on a nail in the wall. He wasn't too red for a victim of sunstroke. He looked at his teeth, pulled at his cheeks, and said "Bravo". It was at that moment that Nochance arrived, out of breath, with a jug of water, which he hurriedly placed at his feet. Bruno couldn't help recoiling; the chap was really round the twist. God knows, he'd never begrudged admiration from anyone; on the contrary, but adoration from a Mongol or a hydro-something-or-other seemed a bit over the top. Oh well.

"Will you leave me alone," he said. "I'm going to have a wash and then I'll join you. I should imagine we'll be eating soon?"

"Yes," Nochance said quickly. "Yes, Madame Luce is just stirring the soup. I'll wait for you out there."

And to Bruno's great surprise – since he was getting used to this veneration – he disappeared without further entreaty.

They were all seated at table, except for Luce, who was slowly stirring the soup with a wooden spatula, under Maurice's lubricious gaze and Arlette's kindly one. Loïc and Diane, exhausted as they were by their laughter and farm-labouring or skivvying, chattered languidly from time to time. Nochance was inert in his corner, his head lowered, and a sort of familial peace reigned in the room.

All this time, Arlette had been doing her calculations: there was Luce who appealed to her young son, and who would keep him in the house better than his ankle

154

(because his ankle wasn't going to last for more than a fortnight). Luce was a nice girl . . . they went together really well . . . she could be taught quickly if one could manage to discover which one she was matched up with . . . Not Loïc, for sure, nor the crafty one. And then there was Diane, she was a true good-for-nothing was Diane, she even managed to mess things up, but Arlette felt a sort of indulgence for this great beanpole. She loved a laugh did Diane. She laughed more at her age than most young girls. And Loïc was a really good sort as well. In spite of that, everyone was eating and drinking . . . and the harvesting was finished. Their presence was no longer required. Should she tell them the truth: that the Germans had got as far as Tours without the slightest resistance, and that you could travel anywhere as long as you toed the line with them? What's more, with this Armistice, old René and Edouard, her husband and younger son, would be home soon. And where would she put everyone? No, she had to act. Nevertheless, something made Arlette feel vaguely sad – she would miss them – but she was so unused to having any feelings at all, that she would never have thought of yielding to them.

So all this high society had to go. Tomorrow she would send Nochance to the garage to find a car for them. And once they were on their way, then they'd see for themselves that the war was over and France was occupied . . . They need never know about her little scheme . . . Ferdinand had nearly blown it at the lunch, when he was showing off to his neighbour. Oh, what a crazy woman Diane was all the same . . .

"Gumoh," her father-in-law called from behind her.

She looked at him affectionately: it was useless saying it, a refined man like him, a man like he'd been, was hard to find. Even people like Bruno could have learnt from him. How was she going to send Nochance off tomorrow? How could she make him go and look for a car, which would then take Bruno away with the others? When Meningou got an idea into his head, she told herself, he was completely one-track. Perhaps if she told him his friend would be staying on at the house in any case, everything would work out: he was jealous of the others, and he'd be relieved to see them disappear . . . Even so, it was a shame . . . that Loïc was a really nice man: he looked nice, and he had a nice personality as well. It was refeshing to meet a real man like that. Ah, her poor Réré, her poor Doudou, where were they now, poor things? . . . Arlette, whose life from its beginning had been regulated by lunch and dinner for the hens and looking after the piglets, by the seasons, harvests and fruit-picking time, had an immutable idea of her fate, and was somewhat exhausted by this maelström around her. She closed her eyes for a moment.

When Bruno arrived, hopping mad and bright red in the face, his effect on certain people, particularly Luce, was like a bomb dropping – to others he seemed more like a wet blanket.

"My sweaters, my sweaters,' he was yelling. 'My cashmere sweaters! That imbecile's been throwing cigarette ends into my pullovers now. Three of them are ruined. Honestly . . ." he said leaning towards Nochance, who was visibly confused, "honestly . . . he's either a complete idiot, or he did it on purpose."

"It's their first little quarrel," Diane said to the

assorted company, but in a conciliatory voice. "All young couples have to go through this stage . . . and then they calm down, either in bed, or somewhere else."

"Oh please, Diane. No, no and no. If only you hadn't lumbered me with this moron. . . !"

"Tut tut," Diane said.

But Bruno wasn't listening:

"And furthermore . . . furthermore . . ."

He was stammering with rage. It was then that he caught sight of Luce.

"Well, Luce, you're looking good. You're quite tanned from working in the fields, too. That's really nice to see. I must admit it's nice to get a close look at you . . . I've missed you."

'Me too, Bruno, me too," poor Luce said – she still had bits of straw in her hair and she was sagging at the knees from all the cooking. "Me too, Bruno. You really frightened us, you know."

"That's true," Maurice joined in, with a nasty smile.

"You got a bad dose of sunstroke in the small distance you covered," said Arlette who harboured grudges. "'Tis the first time I seen a sunstroke that's . . . how did you say it, now, Madame Diane?"

"Oh, come now, Arlette," she cried in a reproachful tone that would have sounded better in the bar of the Ritz ". . . come now . . . do call me 'Diane'. You promised me just now. No more 'madame'. Or I'll have to start calling you 'Madame Arlette'."

Her tone was threatening, but Arlette's shrug of the shoulder implied this was the least of her worries.

"Good," she murmured. "What was I saying?"

She turned to Luce who was gripping the spatula and stirring the soup at breakneck speed.

"Tell me, my little Luce, the soup should be hot by now. Is it soup or mayonnaise you're making us?"

"Is she a bad cookery student, then? Bruno asked ironically, moving away towards the fire.

"Ghee-maw, ghee-maw," brayed the old man, who had not noticed Bruno's arrival till then, and was energetically excusing himself.

It must be said that this unfortunate old man had been wearing his lungs out all day long in order to greet each harvester politely, and he was done for. But red-faced, dishevelled, and dumb with exasperation, Bruno did not respond.

"You could try to answer him," Arlette said dryly.

"Er, er, ghee-maw, ghee-maw," Bruno said absent-mindedly, and for some reason Arlette became exasperated too.

"Oh, come on. You don't have to make fun of him," she said. "Say "Good day" to him. You can say "Good day", can't you? Eh? Granfer don't say ghee-maw on purpose. I wish you could see that. What do you think? Look, sit down there," she shouted at him dryly.

Bruno sat down heavily and looked around him. On the other side of the table, opposite, there was the famous rustic Don Juan, the aforementioned Maurice, tanned by the sun, his old cotton shirt unbuttoned to reveal his muscular, golden torso, a lock of hair falling in his left eye, and his right eye laughing, his cheeks with their five o'clock shadow: a perfect replica of Lady Chatterley's game-keeper. He was badly shaven, but with his skin texture it put one in mind of a pirate rather than a tramp. A certain type of woman would find this bumpkin very attractive, Bruno suddenly thought. But not the type he would have wanted, the type who liked louts.

"It's true. Madame Henri's right," Loïc said seriously. "Imagine if you couldn't say your ps, ls, rs, ms, which you use without consciously thinking about them. What letters would you miss the most. "C" for example would make life difficult. Let's imagine, Bruno, imagine saying to your mistress at the . . . vital moment. "Did you um? Did you um? I ame. Iss me you uddlesome reature. Did you um?" Perhaps you'd be a great hit, one never knows."

"Leave me out of your little jokes, eh, Loïc, Not only do I not understand them, but I'm proud of it. They don't make me laugh."

"Good. Then what does make you laugh? You tell us? You're not a very funny person, you know, Bruno. Just look. In front of you, you have a woman who is better at being a woman than you are at being a man, and who, in addition, feeds you, entertains you, lodges you, dresses you, welcomes you into her bed. And you have to have the sulks. Ah, how I loathe peevish gigolos."

"My private life is my own affair, Loïc. And you can ask Luce why she welcomes me into her bed, as you phrase it. She'll tell you." Bruno gave a delicate little laugh.

"Oh, don't tell me it's for your nights of passion. You make me laugh. Let me tell you there's not a single gigolo who's kept just for his nights of passion. Be reasonable. Women keep their gigolos for the daytime, to show them off, advertise them, take them out with

159

them. The night is a mere detail . . . what do you think? Women have lovers for their friends' benefit, not for themselves. It's because physical love is in fashion, and supposedly necessary for the body's equilibrium, or the ego's . . . what do I know . . . No, I ask you: isn't it thanks to Freud that gigolos still exist? You and all your brotherhood should erect a statue to Freud, shouldn't you?"

"You ask too many questions, Loic. It will all end badly."

"And you don't ask enough, my dear Bruno. At your age you should be only a question mark hoping one day to mature into a full stop. But, alas, you'll only ever be a small comma, like us, in the great alphabet of time. What I'm saying is beautiful, Diane. Have you happened to notice?"

"Superb," Diane said, "but I don't see in what way I'm a comma." She had always been sensitive about her figure.

"I'm not talking from an aesthetic point of view, my dear. I'm speaking from a temporal viewpoint and on Bruno's behalf, who wants to be a full stop and will therefore end up as a semicolon; that's to say, he'll lack the weight, the gravity, the interest of a full stop. And lack the lightness, subtlety and speed of a comma."

"So all I need do is follow your advice; may I remind you once again, and don't you forget it, my private life is my own affair and mine alone."

But during this last tirade, Loïc had gone. And the only person left to face Bruno's trembling rage was Luce, who was trembling in disarray.

Diane decided to follow Loïc, for she saw a lot of possibilities in his new party game, even more in that she didn't understand it too well. For example, could one deliberately remove certain syllables from someone? That could easily lead to a scandal. On the other hand, the punctuation game was more obvious. There would be leader dots for businessman, exclamation marks for love, question marks in the arts etc, etc. and then quotation marks for idiotic remarks, as usual.

She found Loïc lying in the grass in the meadow where the grave was, or, as Luce would say, "the unfortunate hump where Jean lay". She sat next to him, saying nothing, for he looked like a man who liked being silent, he lay with his arm across his eyes and his face turned away, as if to forbid intrusion. Also, Diane did not really want to talk, nor did she need to raise her voice to make her presence felt, since she was wearing her usual delicious perfume on which Ferdinand himself had remarked at the lunch. "A really hot little number." No, it was extraordinary. She was dying to tell Loïc. She would burst if she didn't tell him. Primarily so they could laugh together about this curious compliment, and, secondly, to impress him. My God, to have awakened erotic longings in an ignorant peasant – at sixty. She had to do it. She wished Loïc would notice it himself . . . she would have to sound amused, caustic, even critical in her telling of it.

"Loïc, I meant to tell you . . . but I never had time with all our imbecilic giggling. My God. Poor Bruno's brain. Imagining himself without rs, js, ts, gs, etc. It must be said that, after losing his sweaters and his mistress, to lose his consonants as well would be really too much. That would be a lot to put up with."

"How d'you mean 'losing his mistress'?"

"Don't you have the impression that Luce is pretty friendly with the handsome Maurice?"

Loïc took a deep breath. He had almost fallen into the trap again. Simply through saying nothing, he had almost admitted this liaison existed and, curiously, he had no wish to do so. Later, in Paris, he thought, it would be these memories that would make Luce Ader's life more bearable, warmer. And perhaps she would prefer them to remain secret.

Hovering above him, Diane continued.

"One must say the local men are really gallant."

"You find them so?"

Loïc was astonished. Apart from Maurice, who was fixated on Luce, he hadn't really seen much of it.

"Well yes. That . . . that harvester today . . . there . . . that Ferdinand . . . the tall . . . big one, you remember? With the moustache . . ."

"I well recall which one was Ferdinand," Loic said. "We got on very well together today."

"Well, can you imagine what he said to me . . ." She stopped and began to laugh . . . "he told me . . . Ah, no . . . I can't . . ."

"Oh, come on, Diane."

"I asked him how he spent his winters in the country. And well, he said to me . . . he said to me . . . oh no . . . it's too wild."

"He said *what* to you?"

"He said: 'No, it's not too long . . . particularly if one has a really hot little number like you in bed'."

Now that she'd said the whole thing in a rush, Diane held her breath, ready to burst into laughter with Loïc. But he didn't laugh.

"And . . ." he said. "Why's that so funny?"

"But listen, listen Loïc, he said that to me as a compliment. Isn't that crazy?"

"No, not at all. Why, Diane? Have you got cold feet?" Loïc's voice was gentle all of a sudden. "No, this man has instinct, that's all. And charm. I can tell you, if I were a woman" – and never had there been less suggestion of homosexuality in Loïc's voice – "if I were a woman, I'd find Ferdinand very attractive."

They fell quiet, like the birds, and the wind, and the sun, and the day. And on the very bright canvas of that summer sky, flights of swallows crayonned marvellous black shapes, symbols, puzzles, then gradually abandoned them – doubtless disappointed by the lack of human understanding – and flew away in a straight line, wings battened down, eyes closed, too high or too low, and most certainly too fast . . . And too close to whatever obstacle they could be seen avoiding at the last moment with a casualness that was as enviable as it was deadly.

Bruno surprised his elders in this friendly situation, and took advantage of it. He seemed not in the least annoyed with Loïc, who was slightly ashamed of his abrupt departure.

"I'm delighted to see you so close," he said without apparent irony. "It gives me a chance to ask you a favour."

Loïc and Diane looked at him in surprise, for he

generally announced his wishes rather like commands, that were more or less as immutable as meteorological phenomena.

"I haven't seen Luce for three days," he said in the manner appropriate to a lover. "I thought that this evening you could perhaps . . . er . . . you could perhaps be kind enough to . . . er . . . change rooms . . . I mean change room partners. If, for example, you would accept Loïc as a sleeping partner rather than Luce, Diane?"

"But of course," Diane said, stunned by the proposal, but she'd answered on an initial reflex, in which she imagined Loïc talking wildly to her in the night: it would be more entertaining than having poor Luce so full of contrition and sighs of remorse – or regret – how was she to know?

Loïc was less sure whether this was what Luce would have wanted, but, short of being extremely rude, could not refuse Diane's company, and, short of being sadistic, could not reveal to Bruno that he was no longer in favour.

"Of course," he said mechanically. "Of course, but . . ."

"Thank you," Bruno said warmly, and vanished.

"Don't look so worried, my dear. I'm not going to rape you!" Diane cried with a peal of laughter. "We're no longer of an age to indulge in such frolics."

Loic, whom this "we" had just aged by ten years, didn't move a muscle, except to smile feebly. After all, Luce was old enough to refuse Bruno, he told himself, but he wasn't truly convinced by it, nor by any amount of commonsense arguments he knew were erroneous.

"Our Maurice isn't going to be very happy," he said simply. "I think he's very smitten with Luce."

"That's what I've noticed, proof or no proof," Diane said, hoping to trap him into saying something.

But Loïc did not reply.

Greatly frustrated, Diane continued. "What's more, it's time she made it up with Bruno. They're not on good terms. Now she can't arrive in New York or go back to Paris – I don't know any longer where it will be – as an unattached woman, while that little lout goes around telling everyone she's dropped him for a farmer. That sort of behaviour's fine in a play or a novel, but in real life, you have to admit, it creates a bad impression."

"Of course you're right, as always, Diane: it would give a bad impression."

And in fact demeaning gossip of this kind would harm Luce's reputation, he repeated obstinately in an attempt to convince himself.

And so it was that Luce, who was about to meet Maurice in the barn, saw Bruno – smiling, seductive and threatening – come into the bedroom she shared with Diane. He took her in his arms and pushed her towards the bed.

At first she let herself be kissed, thinking Diane would arrive and save the situation, then hearing her laugh with Loïc in the next room, she understood everything. She struggled, more through desire for Maurice than distaste for Bruno, with whom the sexual act was merely a brief, necessary ceremony, and an unimportant one. She struggled feebly, then yielded, for after all Bruno was her lover. He had a lover's

165

rights. These things were part of life. It was plain where her duty lay.

She hoped Bruno would fall asleep quickly as he normally did, and she would be able to meet Maurice later. But now he had reconquered his chattel, Bruno lit a cigarette, then another, and began a sarcastic rant about the farm. She lay motionless beside him, responding with "yes .. yes .." in a small voice. Then she feigned sleep, her eyes full of tears.

After their ablutions Diane and Loïc lay down on the same bed, for Loïc's modest proposals had met with vulgar laughter from Diane: they were not *both* going to sleep badly, with her on the bed-base and Loïc on the mattress, for the sake of grotesque conventions. The image of a "very hot little number", conjured up by Sir Ferdinand, bothered Loic for a moment or two, but then he forgot it quite painlessly, for Diane, who appeared coated in night cream and swaddled in three dressing gowns because of the humidity, clearly had no erotic notion of herself that night.

They lay in the dark, talking quietly about the day's events, and Diane giggled loudly as she recalled the saga of Nochance and his cigarettes. They were dozing when the shutters creaked and the window opened. A second later, Loïc felt a hunting gun boring into his neck, and a raucous voice ordered him out of bed.

Maurice Henri had drunk a lot of wine at table, and a lot of Plum while he waited for Luce in the barn. When she failed to arrive, he felt a sudden rage and passion, fomented by the alcohol; he took his gun down from

166

the big room, and rushed to the bedroom occupied by his rival who, as he believed, was raping his mistress. He could never have imagined that Luce could be so lax in sexual matters, nor so dutiful.

He levelled his weapon at the male body lying peacefully under the bedclothes, his anger whetted even more by the calm in the room, which signified he'd arrived too late.

"Keep your mouth shut, you lump of shit!" he murmured. "Shut your mouth, you dirty pig!" he said, while continuously jabbing Loïc in the ear with the gun barrel. Stupefied, Loïc obeyed, apart from one or two useless "but . . . buts".

Diane, who had turned on her side when she heard the noise at the window, was horrified to see this black shadow suddenly appear between the window and the bed.

She had seen the gun glinting in the vague nighttime gloom, she had seen Loïc's eyes, a metre from hers, open wide, then she saw him get out of bed, while the stranger murmured orders and insults. A nightmare, a real nightmare. Planes had machine-gunned them, horses had bolted on them, idiots had raped them, and now criminals were threatening them in the middle of the night. Very curiously she never for a moment thought of Maurice, since she did not know he was Luce's lover, and so credited him only with unavowed desires, and therefore with neither criminal obsession nor jealousy.

Her teeth began to chatter violently against the pillow, she was astonished that the murderer had not noticed her, and thanked heaven for his blindness, regretting poor Loïc. Especially after he'd been on such good form. So jolly. Fancy getting killed by some native when he'd spent his life at the Quai d'Orsay. What would they do to him? Set his feet alight to make him say where their money and their jewels were? Despite the darkness, Diane looked towards the fireplace where she had hidden her safe when they arrived. Of course, Loïc didn't know she'd hidden the stuff there in his room. But if they set fire to his feet in front of her, what would she do? She would have to tell them everything. There were no set conventions for contingencies such as these. Furthermore conventions had had no bearing on anything that had happened to them for three days now.

There was Bruno of course, and Maurice Henri. But how could she warn them?

The weak sound of a voice, which seemed to be coming from the big room, reached her. She got up, shiveringly donned a fourth dressing gown, and slid her trembling foot into the corridor. She had earache from listening so intently – like a gundog. At last she picked up some words from Loïc, whose calm astonished her for a moment, before she grasped their implication: "I assure you, Maurice, it's ridiculous. I was persuaded that Luce . . . that nothing has happened."

"Swear. I has to be sure. I'm going to see for myself if that Bruno's asleep."

And Diane recognized Maurice's voice. An intuition struck her like lightning and she entered the kitchen red with rage.

The two men were sitting in front of the fire, with a bottle of red wine and two glasses at their feet, as well as the hunting gun.

168

"My God, Diane, you frightened me," Loic said stupidly. "At this time of night."

"Not me. At this time of night indeed! The fact that I saw a shadow pointing a gun at my bedfellow and watched him disappear into the corridor doesn't bother me one way or the other."

"Ah, you saw everything? I thought you were asleep," Loïc said in a benevolent which Diane found exasperating.

"No, I wasn't asleep. Yes, I saw it all . . . Yes, I've had enough. No, it's not possible to sleep under these conditions. Yes, I was atrociously worried about you. Whatever got into you, Maurice?"

"He thought Bruno was sleeping next to you," Loïc said.

"Bruno? Bruno? For God's sake, what a weird idea he has of the way we behave, that boy. Can you tell me what I'd be doing in bed with Bruno at my age? Nochance's delirium must be catching. Why should anyone wish scabrous relations on me with that cheapskate gigolo? It's inconceivable . . ."

She paced back and forth.

"But . . . but . . . but . . ." the two men stammered, as they were confronted by this Fury, whose scrawny figure in its four dressing gowns gave her the appearance of a prize fighter in training.

"I explained myself badly," Loïc finally said. "He mistook you for Luce."

"Me? . . . Luce?"

She looked at Maurice Henri, hesitating, vaguely flattered.

"In the dark," Loïc said, "it's quite excusable."

169

"Oh no, no! No!' she cried. "No, it's not excusable. Since when has it been all right to enter people's bedrooms in the dead of night with a gun? Are you putting on a performance of *Adrets' Inn* because it's dark, Maurice Henri?"

"Adrets' Inn?" Maurice repeated. "Never heard of it."

"It's a figure of speech. It was a melodrama. Leave it, Maurice. Can't you see, dear Diane, that Maurice is – all straight and above board of course – jealous of Luce, and that . . .

"All straight and above board? You've got to be joking."

"I belong to Luce, you see," Maurice said brusquely, ". . . and since she agreed, I told myself that tonight . . . we'd meet, d'you see, in the same place, but not for long . . ."

"All straight and above board, of course," Diane quipped with a contemptuous glance at Loïc, who looked away.

"I'm fed up. I don't want your Bruno pestering her. I wants to talk to her all alone tonight. There you has it. And I wants her for always."

"That would appear difficult to me," Loïc began, pouring himself a glass of wine, for Maurice was emptying the bottle and it was clearly making him angrier.

Diane caught Loic's look, and picked up Maurice's glass as he put it down on the table for the nth time.

"If you don't mind, I'm dying of thirst."

She filled it and emptied it in one go, giving Loïc a wink, intended to convey the message "One less for

170

him", but from her self-satisfied look, it rather seemed to be saying, "One more for me."

In the meantime, Maurice Henri's eyes, which were normally so good-natured and full of happiness, were bloodshot (or wine-shot) and they now stared at Loïc, then Diane, in black rage, which was more and more disquieting.

"What do you want me to do?" Diane asked. "They're asleep . . . Naturally, they're asleep, Loïc, aren't they?"

She hesitated between two solutions: claiming the friendship between Bruno and Luce was platonic, which would have calmed Maurice down, but left the field open for him to go and awaken his mistress, or to announce the unfortunate truth, which risked enraging him still further and sending him into the lovers' bedroom with a gun. She glanced at Loïc, who appeared to have turned to stone. It must be said that after living with the gun in his ear for five long minutes, he was probably relatively indifferent to Bruno's eventual fate. The blood would not be flowing normally in his veins yet. It was amazing that he had not had a heart attack just now. Or indeed at any time during the last three days.

"I'm going to look for her," Maurice said.

He got up, not without difficulty, and picked up his gun from the floor.

"No, no, no, no. No!" Diane cried. "I repeat Maurice Henri, no!"

"All right, you go and fetch her."

"Ah yes . . . And under what pretext may I ask?"

"Bugger me," said Maurice Henri with a touching sincerity. "Just hurry."

171

"Would this be the ransom for your hospitality?" Diane asked tentatively, but the boy's stony stare gave her to understand that the sacred laws of hospitality had nothing to do with this evening.

"Loïc," she sighed, "you do it. But what can one say? What excuse can one give to wake our friends?"

She had her piercing daytime voice, and, in fact, found it difficult to return to her former emotional state.

"Ah, I quit . . ." she said as if to herself. With a sorrowful countenance, she ostentatiously filled a glass, and swallowed the contents. Nevertheless, her voice had awoken Loïc from his solitary reverie, a common failing with those who'd just escaped assassination.

"Ask Luce to come here," he said. "And if Bruno isn't asleep, pretend I snore too much and you need to sleep next to your usual companion. I'll go and lie next to him a bit later."

"And what if I disturb them . . .?" Diane began. But faced with Maurice's look of hatred, she pointed out: "I mean . . . if they're playing cards, what should I do?"

She panted, she beat the air with her arms, and consequently with eight sleeves, like a sea bird caught in tar.

"Oh well, confiscate their cards," Loïc joked grossly.

"In any case, bring Luce back with you, yes?" the gentle peasant (now turned rutting farmer) added. Maurice Henri was a Jekyll and Hyde character and no mistake.

"I'm on my way," she said.

She rose, and with dragging steps, but holding herself

172

very erect as if she were expecting a discharge of buckshot, she got as far as the door, then suddenly came back:

"Maurice," she said in a dramatic voice: "Maurice, would you allow me a quiet word with my friend Loic?"

"Do what you want, but get a move on," Maurice said, walking towards the alcove and shrugging his shoulders.

Loïc took a few steps towards Diane, and nose to nose, she whispered rapidly: "Come on . . . what do I look like going from bed to bed offering obscene advice to poor Luce. Come on, Loïc. What's your opinion? What do we look like, I ask you?"

"Nothing," Loïc said calmly. "Nothing. We've looked like nothing for the last three days. The day before yesterday and yesterday, we looked vaguely like harvesters. Now I don't know any more . . . and that's the truth."

"Yes, yes, of course," she whispered as she moved off. In the dark she managed to find the door of her ex-bedroom, and make her way to Luce's side of the bed; she held out her hand as she heard her breathing, placed it on her shoulder and patted her affectionately.

"Luce, Luce, wake up."

She patted the shoulder to no avail. Exasperated by this submissive, if not satisfied, woman's regular breathing, she pinched her, but harder than intended.

"My God! Who did that? What's the matter with you?" Bruno wailed, rubbing his neck.

And he lit the lamp on the rickety crate which served

173

as a bedside table. Thanks to which he discovered Diane Lessing ten centimetres from his pillow, tottering and enormous like a Russian doll. *Diane Lessing*, glistening with night cream, her eyes popping out of their sockets.

He jumped.

"Oh come off it, Diane. What're you doing here?" he enquired, well-meaningly at first.

Then, after several moments of obstinate silence, he noticed her tightened jaw and her pallor, and a kind of doubt, a kind of reassurance began to suggest a more pleasant hypothesis. In a low voice, for Luce was in fact still fast asleep by his side, he whispered:

"But – you hurt me, Diane. What d'you want me for? If it's what I think it is, you've come a bit late."

And he cackled, half astonished, half amused. In any case, well pleased with this nocturnal flame in the old Lessing, who was listening to him with eyes lowered. But now she reacted and looked up:

"What? What did you say? What *are* you thinking of?" she yelped.

"What are *you* thinking of?" Bruno repeated, laughingly imitating her. "You tell me what you're doing, Diane, if you please, half-lying on top of me, in the middle of the night. And at this hour?"

"I beg your pardon? What *do* you believe? You imagine me running after you like a bitch on heat? In the middle of the night? You're mad. Ahah," she guffawed, with effort. "Me running after 'that'?" she said to an invisible audience and pointing to Bruno Delors sitting up in bed with the lascivious, triumphant look of a Regency buck.

"Then, why won't you let 'that' sleep?" he demanded. "Why pinch 'that'? Eh, Diane? D'you hear me? Eh?"

And he stood up, sarcastic and implacable, and posed to show off his handsome torso, breathing deeply; the young spurned male before a Diane Lessing twisting her hands in desire, shame and despair. Such was the idea he formed of the situation, but it was not to last for long.

"Loïc," Diane shouted, in a piercing voice. "Loïc, come here."

The door swung open violently, and Loïc, his hair awry and pale, made his entrance, flanked by Maurice Henri, red in the face and armed with a double-barrelled shotgun which he was waving all over the place.

"A nightmare! Tonight is just a long nightmare," Diane said to her friend Loïc as she threw herself into his arms.

"Ah yes, a nightmare. You said it," Bruno repeated without any sense of gallantry, while Luce half-awake, turned towards Bruno in her sleep, and tenderly stretching out her hand, cried in a low but distinct voice:

"Maurice, my Maurice."

There was then a very long, real silence. Made even longer by the fact that no one felt immediately capable of breaking it.

Naturally it was Diane who took up the reins.

"Bruno," she said from her superior position after thirty years of society gossip and tricky situations of this nature – and she coughed – "Bruno," she began again, in a precise, arrogant, clear voice, "I was expecting to find Luce on this side of the bed where she has slept

175

till now. I am truly sorry, dear Bruno, for raising your false hopes," she said cynically. "In fact, would you be an angel . . . in view of Loïc's snoring, would you kindly go back to your old room, and give me back mine, so that I can get a bit of sleep. So that both myself and Luce can get some sleep?"

The three men looked at each other. Finally two of the men looked at the third with his gun and tiptoed from the room, their faces impenetrable, pale and silent.

After three minutes had passed while she took off two of her dressing gowns, lay down, brought the sheets up to her chin and sighed violently without the least explanation, Diane Lessing turned to Luce, who seemed to be having a cataleptic fit, with her eyes wide open.

"Luce, my dear, 'someone' is waiting for you, outside, I believe. Be sweet and get there at the gallop, and don't wake me when you come back. Good night, Luce."

Having said that, Diane immediately dived into the arms, the only arms other than Ferdinand's that could have satisfied her longing that night: the arms of Morpheus.

Chapter 9

Nochance had been assigned a mission which would at last leave Bruno to his blandishments, and rid him of Bruno's friends, who were preventing him from giving positive expression to a multitude of very lubricious desires. At dawn, he set out for the village of Mézouy-les-Tours, which boasted the only garage to repair and hire cars in the whole region.

In those troubled times M. Silbert, the proprietor, was disposing of an old limousine which had been used for weddings, funerals and other functions such as Great War Veterans' reunions, fishing and hunting club outings. The limousine must have been ten or fifteen years old and, as Silbert told Nochance – after he'd absorbed his message – it was worth ten thousand francs, take it or leave it. That this ultimatum existed was due entirely to the ignorance and folly of city-dwellers in general and these ones in particular, whose presence at the Henris was known by the garage owner and the whole of the surrounding district. To cut a long story short, the phrase "Take it or leave it" was written on a piece of paper along with the origins, life history and price of the car, and confided to Nochance, who made a more reliable courier than he did a spokesman. He set out again at the same speed, found a cart halfway along the road which welcomed him aboard, and arrived back at midday in time for lunch. Nochance was as devoted and tail-wagging as a retriever would have been, had it carried the message all the way back in its mouth, and he immediately delivered the missive to Arlette. He then set off in search of his handsome Bruno, whom he found where he had left him fast asleep; he was still fast asleep.

What had happened was that the resident cock, who'd been oblivious of the night's disturbances after his hoarseness of the previous day, had begun crowing as soon as it was dawn. His cock-a-doodle-doos were soon accompanied by the ghee-maw-ghee-maws of Granfer in full cry, and the chorus swelled by the cackles of hens making pompous predictions as they pattered round the house: all, however, were quite blasé about the noise they were creating.

Unable to sleep, Luce and Diane, and then Loïc, had joined Arlette in the kitchen and had vaguely helped her prepare the feed for the animals. Having volunteered to distribute it in her stead, the two women set off briskly for the other yard, where the geese where rampaging about.

Loïc and Arlette had just finished feeding the pigs a good five minutes later, when the sound of running feet and honking made them turn back. Elbow to elbow, Diane and Luce were being chased by a good half-dozen hopping-mad ganders, some accompanied by their equally outraged females. Armed with a stick and an old broom, Arlette and Loïc pitched into the angry flock, while the two women, who had run for safety up the entrance steps, energetically refused to come down.

"Whatever happened then?" Arlette asked between cries of "Son of a whore" and great swipes with her washboard at the geese, who were coming for them with necks outstretched.

"It's like d'Artagnan and Athos fending off Richelieu's henchmen, two against eight," Loïc said as he brandished his broom before him. "On guard, you Cardinal's lackeys. Take that, unfortunate Sire. On guard, on guard. I lunge, cut over, press, parry . . . oh shit, he's bitten me. That bastard's bitten me," he cried. And he threw the broom at it. But luckily, the geese, perhaps overcome by remorse, surged back to their pen.

"Bloody slags," Arlette muttered, all red in the face.

And, as always when faced with this rare coarse language, the three Parisians adopted a semi-deaf, semi-offended expression – for they still found it necessary to respect whatever it was that made them obey.

"Show me what she done to you, the whore. Ah, no. 'Twas a gander what did that," she corrected herself immediately.

Loïc was astonished:

"How can you tell? Is there a difference between a gander's teeth and a goose's? Or does the male peck deeper? In contrast to our European customs, where the female is the deadlier, isn't that so, Mesdames? My God, I'm going to bleed to death if this continues."

And, in fact, blood was pouring profusely down his shirt. The two women quickly came down from their perch and hurried towards him, while Arlette

179

mumbled to deaf ears, "My word. Whatever got into those creatures? Them ganders don't normally act like that. 'Tis the first time since I had them I seen them run. The geese, yes. They gets daft when they'm on heat, but the ganders, never. Never." And she went on shaking her head. Luce had adopted a dramatic expression, and Diane was asking herself out loud and at speed, how a haemorrhage could be staunched, which awakened Loïc's verve in spite of his wound.

"'A gander kills one of our representatives from the Quai d'Orsay'. What a wonderful newspaper headline. 'It was while defending his two geese that Loïc Lhermitte was killed by a rival'. That seems to ring true to me – very convincing I'd say . . . Of course I have no one particular in mind . . . you do believe me, Mesdames? Unless Bruno has something of a gander about him in the way he sticks his nose in the air. I know I'm drivelling on, but I'm afraid that if I stop, I'll faint."

They took him back to the house and sat him in the famous alcove, where they rigged up some sort of tourniquet. The old man was quiet, since he was intrigued, and Arlette could not stop worrying.

"I'm going to get my earth from outside," she said. "I don't have none indoors. I'll be back. Keep him tied up. Don't move from here."

She ran off.

"What a wonderful woman," Loïc said. "She's even gone to fetch one of her special cobwebs. What a good woman she is. Now, tell me what really happened? What did you do to those creatures?"

180

"It . . . it was Diane," Luce began fearfully. "It was Diane . . . she . . . isn't that right Diane?"

"Oh, I really don't give a damn what you say," Diane said casually, "as long as it's not in front of Arlette. Go on, tell him, my dear."

"Well, it was like this," Luce whispered. "When Diane saw all the geese together in their pen . . . honestly, they did look a bit stupid . . . she tried imitating them. She stood on her right leg and with her left leg held out behind, and her arms raised, and waved them up and down. It did look exactly like them . . . From the front she looked like a letter T, d'you see?"

"I see," Loïc laughed. "And it will perhaps be my last vision before I fall into a coma . . . And then? What happened? They didn't like this T, I take it?"

"No, I don't think it was that," Luce said, shaking her head thoughtfully like a psychologist. "No, it was when Diane started imitating their call that everything went wrong."

"How was that?"

"Oh, she did it terribly well," Luce acknowledged with a hint of surprise and admiration in her bitterness. "She started making their call, but it was absolutely identical. Do it again, Diane, just to show Loïc."

"Careful, careful," Diane whispered. "If Arlette suspected . . ."

She glanced towards the corridor, then towards the entrance to the house and let out a harsh cry, a hissing, stupid cry, so similar to the geese five minutes earlier that Loïc shivered.

"It's fantastic. It's so like them, you're absolutely

right. And they didn't like that? Perhaps you said something pretty offensive to them without knowing?"

"Yes, it must have been that," Luce agreed. "It must have been. All at once, they went completely berserk. And I'd thought their pen was closed. They came rushing out and started trampling all over us. One pecked my foot so hard I screamed to Diane to run for it. And so that's just what we did . . . But," she continued in a tone that was both plaintive and aggressive, "how could we have quietened them down once they'd been let loose? Remember the cry, you must do it, too," she said with a sombre pride.

"It's not difficult," Diane said modestly. "You make the cry from the back of your throat, you half-close your teeth, push your tongue forward, and that's it . . ."

This time she started to do it much louder. And the other two jumped and looked behind them, but Arlette must have had to go right to the back of the barn to find her cobwebs or her special soil.

"I was really frightened," Luce went on, shaking her head. "I've not felt so frightened for months."

"They looked so stupid," Diane repeated, with a persistent arrogance. "They were standing there on their great webbed feet, their throats all puffed up with anger, with their tiny hateful eyes, and fat stomachs. They looked just like a bunch of old bankers. I can't tell you . . . they were hid-eous. Hideous and hateful. Ah, dirty creatures. And I'm not altogether displeased I . . . insulted them, am I? I'm not sure, but I did feel disturbed and angry. Yes, and so much the better!"

"You can feel even less displeased, Diane dear, that it wasn't you who had to carry the can!" Loïc moaned mournfully, holding out his bloody arm. "It's always others who pay for your follies, Diane, I don't know if you've noticed. But this feels terrible. Terrible."

For once, Diane took a hint and showed the closest signs yet to remorse (though they still had a long way to go).

"I *am* sorry. Truly sorry, Loïc. If you think about it. If you hadn't been there, those creatures would have torn us limb from limb, wouldn't they, Luce?"

"'Two society women torn limb from limb by ganders. No longer a question of jealousy, but savage desire motivating this new drama!' Loïc declaimed, as he described the catastrophe in his imaginary role as editor in chief.

"All that blood," Diane said.

"Don't drown in remorse, Diane. No. If you want to console me, you can swear me an oath . . ."

"Whatever you wish."

"Swear to me that you'll do me a gander's call whenever I ask . . . in Paris or no matter where else and at no matter what party, whenever I ask. At any time in the next year, let's say."

"A gander's call . . . And well, yes . . . um. I don't know if . . . um what about if the King of England was there or some other important person?"

But Loïc's severe expression and his arm removed all her defences.

"All right. Agreed. A year."

"And you won't forget?"

"What?"

"The gander's call. I personally shall never forget you making it."

183

"Yes, yes, of course. When I promise, I promise," Diane said, although a little crestfallen in spite of everything, and anguished. In her imagination, she half saw a huge dinner party with very important guests, Loïc discoursing till out of sight on his syllables and consonants, with no one understanding anything, Luce with her mindless expression, Bruno recounting his rape by a halfwit in the Beauce countryside, and herself making gander calls. Yes – they would make a grand team. They'd be invited everywhere, but never invited again.

Arlette arrived with Maurice, her bizarre pharmacy tucked under her arm, and a strange, almost frightened look on her face.

Diane couldn't help sighing.

"What've you got to sigh about?" Loïc enquired.

"I was wondering what the past has in store for us?" she said absentmindedly.

But, strangely, no one commented on this lapse. Not even Loïc as they dressed his wound and put him in the shade, his three Fates grouped around him.

The animals were quiet, harvesting was over – all was safely gathered in – there were no more guests for lunch, and so they could relax a little in the open air, with their feet in the sun and their heads in the shade, in that silence which had been so disquieting to begin with, and was so pleasant now. This silence of the fields that they now knew emanated from a land suffocating under the sun, from birds preoccupied with finding food, from trees whose leaves hung motionless for want of a breeze. After the violent scenes with the

184

poultry, it was a delicious calm, although Arlette had refused Diane the small glass of Plum she claimed necessary for her nervous system. This peace lasted only an instant, for they soon noticed that Arlette's eyes – which they usually saw fixed on some household object or the horizon – had, as she gazed at their three faces, taken on expressions of shame and despotism, which were both fleeting and contradictory in equal measure. Loïc reacted in his usual manner and tried to banish this cloud with a remark.

"Can a gander be more stupid than a goose?" he asked them all. "Do you know that collection, Diane? It's very, very fine. They're poems by Paul Eluard . . . the title differs slightly from my version . . . but the musicality is much the same."

"It reminds me of something," Diane said amiably, for even if she didn't know something, she always claimed, with all cultural references, that they "always reminded her of something", which made her feel affable.

"It was a very beautiful collection that . . ."

He stopped. It was impossible to deflect Arlette from one of her moods when she happened to have one. It was too rare an event for it to be without significance or consequence.

"Arlette," he said. "You're looking worried. What's the matter?"

Arlette Henri opened her mouth, shut it again, crossed her hands on her knees.

"The matter? . . . Well . . . 'tis like this – when you arrived, we asked at the garage, if there were a car for you . . . Seeing that . . . seeing that no one thought that . . . the farm . . . you wouldn't be staying even three hours, eh, from the look of you."

"One might well have thought that," Diane said smiling. "Essentially, this wasn't a holiday for us. But I'm going to astonish you, my dear Arlette . . ."

She leant across and placed her hand on her hostess's wrist which she then patted several times with great enthusiasm and sincerity.

". . . I'm going to astonish you: I've never felt so well anywhere before . . . I've never felt so fit as here. Not in Gstaad, nor Haiti, nor Davos, nor Le Touquet, nowhere. It's curious."

"And so, what about the car?" Loïc's voice was steady, but tauter than Diane's. And Luce had gone pale under her country tan, so different from a seaside tan (in fact, far prettier) Diane had noted.

"Well . . . it seem there is one. I'd forgotten about it, things being as they was. And now all the roads is safe, and the Germans has gone back to their own country, the man at the garage have said he have one.

"I sent Nochance to do some errands at the saddler's," she stammered. "And Silbert gave him this . . . for you." She held out a dirty piece of paper to Loïc, turning away to avoid his eyes. But he had seen panic change her features and give her a fleeting, unexpected, curiously embarrassing femininity.

He said nothing.

"But you can take your time, of course," she said. "I'm not going to throw you out, am I? No. That would be . . . that would be something," she almost moaned.

And under her guests' wide-eyed stares, she lifted

186

up her apron, bent over and hid her face in it, in the manner of a Greek widow or a naughty schoolgirl.

"But what's going on?" Diane cried, standing up. "My dear Arlette. What's happening? What's the matter with you? Have you had some bad news? Are your husband and son all right?"

"Oh yes, they'm fine, really fine," Arlette's stifled voice replied, as she suffocated from the heat in her apron and was astonished with herself for stupidly not daring to emerge from her refuge.

"Well, it's the principle of the thing. If they're alive, they'll be coming home. They'll be here very soon. Isn't that right, Arlette? But I'm here, I'm here."

And, all excited and delighted with her perspicacity, Diane turned to her friends.

"It's that. Of course. I know what it is. They're coming back and you won't know where to put us. It's that? Ah, my dear Arlette, what a child you are. Really. In any case we have to leave: the harvesting's finished," she said in a logical tone, as if Loïc, Luce, Bruno and herself had been qualified itinerant farmhands for hire. "We have to get back, too. Why worry about nothing. Dear Arlette, I know that you would keep us if you could."

"Dear Arlette" seemed less and less willing to abandon her apron.

"I'm sure the car is all ready for our departure. Here, give me that note, Loïc. What d'you think of that: 'Take it or leave it'. We'll take, it of course. It's not much, is it, Loïc?"

"I don't know if we'll be able to get as far as Paris in a 1927 Delage," Loïc said, "but we'll have a go."

187

"Of course it's not the Chenard. But we're not exactly snobs, are we? We'll arrive in the Champ-Elysées in our Delage, like proper tourists . . . And dear Arlette, that's enough tears. We'll come back and see you very, very soon. And you could come to Paris. We could have lunch together. In the restaurant of your choice," she said, with diminishing enthusiasm. "Or better still at my flat. But have we got time now to have a bite? I imagine they won't arrive before nightfall, since that's the usual time."

"How d'you know what time soldiers return home?" Loïc asked faintly.

"I don't know, but in films or plays, I've always noticed that soldiers or musketeers arrive home at night. It must correspond to something? Mustn't it? Then, we've time to have lunch together, haven't we, Arlette?"

Arlette nodded vigorously, with her head still under her apron.

"You see, Loïc?"

Diane was triumphant, but alone in being so. Loïc stood up and walked towards the coomb. And Luce was weeping openly, sitting motionless in her chair, despite Bruno's and Maurice's arrival.

From instinct Loïc went to sit in the same meadow as on the previous evening. Where he'd joked with Diane, where he'd made some complimentary remarks on her physical appearance. Extravagant. No, he was a nice chap when he thought about it, and a nice sentimental chap if he thought about it some more, for, when it came to it, he would be the only one who was sad to leave this place, except for Luce, of course. Luce, who had encountered the friendly reassuring face of love, which had been so necessary to her. At last she had found the possibility of happiness or serenity. And even her tears showed a certain effortlessness in the way she could cry, a facility in crying, and yielding to feelings, which augured well for the future. He had known her when she was incapable of manifestations of this kind, and she was no longer like that. As for Bruno, this place where he'd been humiliated should give him itchy feet. This farm had punished him well, and that wasn't so bad, was it? Besides his sunstroke and his love affair, he'd lost a little of his arrogance during his ordeal . . .

As for himself, Loïc would miss a place where he'd felt at ease, that was all. But after this disappointment about the length of their stay, which was a childish disappointment, then, he had only one wish: to leave, to flee this place, leave this grass, this meadow where he'd felt so stupidly, naïvely and gently in harmony with life . . . with his life . . . with his caricature of life.

That sunset the previous day which had left him so serene, so close to happiness, was once again just one of those naïve, cruel colour prints from Epinal, he'd leafed through when young and long forgotten, an image that he had, sometimes deliberately, sometimes masochistically, blotted out with the clear, honest perspective of his own deep-rooted rationality, barely tinged with bitterness. He had of course allowed himself to lapse into these lyrical extensions of his own existence. He had added lights, candles, flowers, and music, and had abandoned himself to his flood of fantasies. But in

189

more grandiose circumstances all the same. On long journeys for instance . . . or for a very secret woman. He had never thought he could yield and allow himself to feel optimism, or serenity, or happiness on a small, somewhat squalid farm, two hundred kilometres from Paris. And on an unhappy weekend made up of the most unexpected events. But now the time had come for him to put on his anti-cloud, anti-Society armour again, his bullet-proof, ball-proof armour of irony – it was just a precaution like any other. But like all precautions, it ended up almost causing its user's downfall, and leading him astray, but less disastrously than if he not resorted to it at all.

Dear Arlette didn't pull her punches, Diane thought; until now no one had ever despatched her in such a manner from any château in France or Navarre. She was of course still somewhat vexed by it, but more astonished than anything else. Arlette should have spoken to her about it first. After all, they were both "leaders" in this strange team, the two in charge. Even if her men *were* coming home, there was no need to make them clear out at this speed, on the very same day . . . Not that she, Diane, would ever have imagined staying more than a week in this place. But it was unpleasant to have to rush in this way. Anyway. Perhaps Arlette had found them a bit of a burden? Perhaps peasants such as these with their poultry, flies and braying grandfather found the cream of Parisian high society something of an irritant? That would have been comical. No, it had to be something else. But what was it? Had they offended Arlette or made her feel excluded? No, she would have known immediately. Even with people as different in their behaviour, education and sentiments as these peasants, Diane felt an awakening intuition, a sort of power of divination which was never wrong: she noticed everything. It only needed the smallest detail to be not quite right and she would immediately suss it out. This constant, excessive receptiveness and sensitivity, on which people never ceased to congratulate her, could even be exhausting at times. She, Diane, would occasionally have loved to see nothing and hear nothing. She would have loved to be impassive like some great ruminant animal, with its eyes wide open, just like so many others.

In the meantime, the only explanation for this rushed departure had to be the return of the two soldiers. For a diplomat who'd been unemployed for a week, it might seem too facile an answer, perhaps, but it was the only one . . . so Loïc had better resign himself to it.

Their return to Paris would be less triumphant than Diane thought, both Arlette and Maurice told themselves in their heart of hearts, for both knew which way the war was heading. But Maurice did not dwell on his vague remorse: he was far more preoccupied with another matter: Luce. Luce was leaving. His beautiful sweet Luce was leaving. His mother could have waited a little longer, or at least warned him.

He cast Luce a desperate look, and to show that he was innocent, cried: "What? What the 1927 Delage? You couldn't say 'twill even get to Tours. And then, have the firing stopped? Yes?"

Luce's pale white face, her small frightened submissive face tore at his heart. He smiled at her but she lowered her gaze. It was clear she expected no more of him than of other men. And Maurice Henri, despite all his natural flexibility, felt like lead, a brute. Never would he find a woman who gave him so much pleasure, nor a woman to whom he could give so much pleasure either. And the very obvious admiration in Luce's eyes, her brilliant eyes as she lay in the hay, the way she'd moved her hand along his back, his hips, his chest, his neck, with a simple, ecstatic slowness, all of it already made him want to cry. She was his woman. She was his possession . . . And never had a woman so manifestly, so physically appeared to belong to him. This couldn't be allowed to happen. He walked over to her and took her by the elbow, but, with no reproach and apparently no tears, she averted her eyes and turned her head away.

"It doesn't matter," she said weakly ". . . I knew quite well that . . . but it's all happened so quickly."

He too looked down, and clumsily tried to take her hand in his, in front of everyone. And nobody moved. No one seemed to have noticed anything. Bruno even less than the others.

"Only a war could transform a 1939 Chenard-Walcker into a 1927 Delage," Diane remarked.

"I can't believe it'll get us as far as Paris," Loïc said, "but it will take us some of the way."

"Don't you believe it. Those cars are indestructible. We'll be in Paris in three hours at the most, especially since the Germans have unblocked the roads. There'll only be refugees. We might do better going on the smaller roads." Bruno was jumping for joy. He couldn't conceal his happiness, though he was trying to. For everyone found Luce's misery more moral and more dignified than his gaiety – even though she had deceived him with an absolutely cynical sleight of hand, such as exists in this world.

He would see she was punished for it later in Paris. Until then, nothing must hinder their departure. He was exultant. At first he did not feel Nochance's hand patting him on the shoulder, but he turned round at last, and even smiled at the idiot in his joy.

"You, be not worried," Nochance whispered, as he spluttered disagreeably into his ear. "You not to worry. You staying."

"That's right. On a diet of cold water!" Bruno replied in a schoolboy reflex. And he laughed.

"All arranged with Arlette," Nochance confirmed. For a moment, a terrible moment, Bruno panicked. Surely they weren't going to leave him here, tied to a chair, to the mercy of this perverted half-wit? They were the ones who liked the countryside, not him. He sidled up to Arlette who, like everyone else, appeared to be busy, putting tools away or cutting flowers, goodness knows what.

"What's this tale your workhand's telling me? That you want me to stay?"

"Ah, there's no risk of that!" Arlette said with a firmness which, though reassuring, annoyed him at the same time. "There's no risk of that, but let him believe it, otherwise he's going to make a big scene. But, anyway, I'll send him over to the Faberts before you leave."

"Agreed," Bruno said hurriedly.

It was going to be jolly at the farm this evening. The Henris had something of a treat in store, with the idiot howling at the moon and their grandfather braying his ghee-maws, till the cock began his early morning chorus.

"So?"

Nochance was now dogging his steps, screwing up his eyebrows – if that is what one could call the velvety horizontal bar which joined his ears together.

"So, she told you?"

"Yes, yes, my old comrade, she told me, and everything's all right. I'll go with my friends as far as the crossroads, and then I'll leave them after, so I can keep you company here, and toil away in the fields."

"You don't have to work, you know," Nochance murmured, who except on great occasions was always idle. "And anyway, harvesting's finished."

"I'm sure you'll find us something to do. I shan't worry about it," Bruno said jubilantly.

Neither one or the other had noticed the unexpected development in their language, but Loïc could not help noticing Bruno's disfiguring sense of superiority and contempt. For a second he concentrated on him all the vague revulsion and fear this return to the capital had engendered.

"Stop making fun of that poor chap," he cried. "You'll be loved by a lot worse than him."

Chapter 10

And so, once again, everyone was seated for lunch in the big room, their moods being both solemn and capricious.

"What are we having to eat?" Diane asked, having obviously decided to be life-and-soul of the party, and to keep up this role right to the end.

"Ganders – ganders in blood," Loïc suggested bitterly.

"No, nobody don't eat that," Nochance, the bashful lover, said. "And nobody don't kill ganders neither . . . because of the geese."

"What d'you mean, 'because of the geese'?"

"The geese wants the ganders come springtime, isn't that right, Maurice?"

"Ghee-maw," Granfer brayed, because all at once his grandson seemed to have a quite different preoccupation on his mind – the beautiful young girl.

"Yes, come springtime, you don't have to take the gander to the geese, the geese is so keen," Nochance assured them once again. And sifting through his thoughts, he added: "'Tis a bit like with us . . . eh?" Whereupon he burst into one of his hearty, hideously obscene laughs which, as usual, gave everyone the shivers.

Loïc lit a cigarette, and leant his chair back. It had to be said he looked more like a painter or a dropout than a diplomat, with his longish hair hanging over his collar and forehead.

From time to time Diane looked at him anxiously. She didn't know why, but, for the last hour or two, ever since the saga with the ganders, Loïc Lhermitte disturbed her. Something didn't "gell". And yet, like them, he ought to be happy to be going back to Paris.

He began a final diatribe: "These similarities between species," he said in his lazy, day-dreamy voice, "are always interesting . . . If you take the parallel Nochance pointed out for instance . . . this sexual ardour . . . the way one species will refuse any hint of prevarication in springtime, and another refuse it all year round. These sexual demands are curious, aren't they? However, such comparisons aren't always to your advantage, ladies . . ."

The "ladies" – one surprised, one critical, the third blank – turned to look at him.

"What are you talking about, then?" Diane asked.

"I'm talking about devotion: think of the number of geese, of those poor young things killed every year, every generation . . . the way they're just put in a cold narrow steel can, separated from their family surroundings . . . until we eat them. Have you a friend or relative, Diane, who'd put up with that, knowing that her gander-husband, who's been left behind, will forget her in the arms (or the feet, I should say) of another silly goose? Ah no, I'd be astonished if you had."

196

"Honestly, he's gone completely round the bend," Diane said with conviction. "Whatever's got into you, Loïc? What *are* you talking about?"

"I'm talking about the comparison between you and the geese, which Nochance started most intelligently."

"Sometimes I really wonder what you get up to at the Quai d'Orsay."

"I help create wars," Loïc said spiritedly. "The last little one started off very well. There was an over-equipped, bellicose nation, pitted against a totally shambolic, scatterbrained country called France. It could have lasted for years. No. I really do wonder what has happened? Well, nothing in politics is ever reliable, not even in the worst sort of politics."

And, with a great sigh, Loïc picked up the bottle of chilled wine and poured generous glasses for his neighbours, not forgetting himself.

Hardly had he had time to put the bottle down and empty his glass, than they were holding out their glasses for more. It seemed that either a great thirst or a new shyness had descended on their happy family: like an embarrassment, a sort of belated recovery of their identity, as though each had labels stuck to their backs for their departure: "Diplomat, assumed to be homosexual" for Loïc; "Gigolo aged twenty-eight" for Bruno, "Frightfully busy Society woman" for Diane, "Young, rich, unhappily married woman" for Luce. And everyone was trying to recapture their own personality, or rather, attempting to reintegrate it with the others, to regain their self-esteem. And each of them found the other three ridiculous, and, at odd moments,

197

touching in their desire to ressemble themselves, or at least their Parisian selves.

"I'm really going to miss this little wine," Loïc said, addressing Arlette, who nodded to show she had registered the compliment.

There was much to-ing and fro-ing between "bedrooms" and the "car": terms which generally denoted something more luxurious, and which were comic when one saw their actual state. Then everything seemed to happen very quickly and very slowly at the same time: there was the excessive physical effort involved in carrying the luggage from one to the other, Diane protesting when her suitcase stuffed to the brim with goodness knows what burst in the yard, and the orders, objections, grimaces involved in tying Loïc's and Bruno's suitcases on the roof – since the boot of the Delage couldn't take them. So when they were actually ready to leave, at least on a technical level, they were almost astonished. But now that Arlette could heave a sigh of relief at the thought that they'd soon be gone, she somehow couldn't bring herself to accept it. Now that her duties were over, she asked them quite sincerely to stay for dinner – and then to stay one more night. It would be better to leave early in the morning, she said, than have to have a dreadful overnight journey to Paris. But the die had been cast, Bruno was champing at the bit, Luce's tears were unstoppable, and all this made further delay seem like sadistic cowardice.

"Look," Diane said affectionately, opening her Vuitton suitcase, "Look, Arlette, please. Take this. It will look divine on you."

"This" was a knitted bedjacket – a real cashmere one in pale pink – it was gorgeous, or would have been, except that imagining it wrapped round Madame Memling seemed completely hilarious.

"'Tis very pretty, but what's it used for?" the interested party asked.

"To keep your shoulders warm in winter," Loïc said.

"Ah, that's good, 'tis no joke here when it start getting cold, all those effing thermometers explodes, come wintertime," she said in her somewhat coarse language again, much to her guests' displeasure.

These crude words and the swearwords which only rarely littered her vocabulary, had become conspicuously more frequent since their projected departure.

"Come on then, let's go," Loïc said, as Luce's tears began to distress him.

Thereupon the scene became confused – with everyone throwing their arms around everyone else, except for Bruno, and embraces and goodbyes were so mixed that Diane found herself kissing Loïc with every sign of despair. Once all these effusions had subsided a little, they got into in the car, with Luce and Bruno behind, Loïc at the steering-wheel and Diane beside him. Like a model family, Loïc thought momentarily, with the children in the back and his "Old Missus" beside him. He glanced at his Old Missus, who had wound down her window, and was resting her arm on the sill, ready, he felt, to wave graciously, even send kisses to her peasants. And now that the Parisians were ensconced in their car and out of the yard – "her peasants" once more took on the appearance of country bumpkins, yokels in their worn-out work clothes, with overdone, uneven suntans.

"Well, till we meet again," he cried, and the car shuddered.

Luce had pressed her face against the window and was staring fixedly at her lover, who was gradually disappearing from view, and he too stood stockstill watching them. When they reached the top of the coomb, it was the white blob of her face in the dark car that Maurice continued to follow with his eyes long after it was obliterated in the cloud of dust thrown up on the dusty track.

Naturally the Delage got lost following Arlette's rather rudimentary directions. They were driving in circles and so was a German half-track, which happened to be searching for a few French soldiers who'd decided to go on fighting.

The German vehicle had stopped at the crossroads, and saw the ancient car coming slowly towards them, but not braking.

"What on earth are they up to?" Bruno asked. "Are they looking for Germany?"

"Well," Loïc said, "I've no intention of taking any prisoners today." And he accelerated, to the great astonishment of the German lieutenant, who gave the signal to his machine-gunners – and did it so emphatically, that Diane, either not thinking because she was overtired, or just out of amusement, took a French flag she'd found left in the car by the Great War Veterans and gaily waved it through the window.

Since they were seated in the back, Bruno and Luce

were undoubtedly hit by the first burst of machine-gun fire, and Loïc too, since the car immediately began to slow down and zigzag from one ditch to the other before slewing off the road. There was only one survivor, as the German gunners confirmed, when, after a good minute, they saw her get out of the car, with her cluster of red – almost bright-red – curls, and an extremely angry face, but they had no time to study her in detail before picking her off like a rabbit.

Almost immediately afterwards the car burst into flames.

There was a great deal of difficulty in identifying the victims of this blunder, and it was made worse by the fact that almost nothing remained. It was Ader's influence with German staff headquarters and his numerous enquiries which established the truth. But by then the length of time taken to discover these travellers made it difficult to mourn them as much as was their due; first of all, because there was no actual date of death; and, secondly, no apparent reason for their bizarre demise.

In order to grieve and mourn, you need precise circumstances, and a definite place, details which, thank God, are not required for pleasure and happiness, which can make do with much more blurred parameters.

/

ALLISON & BUSBY FICTION

Phillip Callow
The Magnolia
The Painter's Confessions
Some Love

Catherine Heath
Lady on the Burning Deck
Behaving Badly

Chester Himes
Cast the First Stone
Collected Stories
The End of a Primitive
Pink Toes
Run Man Run

R.C. Hutchinson
Johanna at Daybreak

Dan Jacobson
The Evidence of Love

Francis King
The Widow

Colin MacInnes
Absolute Beginners
City of Spades
Mr Love and Justice
The Colin MacInnes Omnibus

Henry Miller
Quiet Days in Clichy

Adrian Mitchell
The Bodyguard

Bill Naughton
Alfie

Dolores Pala
In Search of Mihailo

Boris Pasternak
Zhenia's Childhood

Ishmael Reed
Reckless Eyeballing
The Terrible Threes
The Terrible Twos

Francoise Sagan
Engagements of the Heart
Incidental Music
The Leash
Those without Shadows
The Unmade Bed

Budd Schulberg
The Disenchanted
Love, Action, Laughter
and Other Sad Tales
On the Waterfront
What Makes Sammy Run!

Debbie Taylor
The Children Who Sleep
by the River

Etienne van Heerden
Ancestral Voices